Two Pairs of Six-inch Heels and One Comfortable Shoe

a novel

Amy E. Reichert

Published by BookLocker.com, Inc., Bradenton, Florida.

Printed in the United States of America on acid-free paper.

The characters and events in this book are fictitious. Any similarity to real persons, living or dead, is coincidental and not intended by the author.

BookLocker.com, Inc.
2014

First Edition

Dedication

This book is dedicated to my partner in all things - Robin L. Bowersock. I admire her ongoing sense of humor, adventure, and support of my projects and plans.

Chapter 1

Here we are, we're starting at the end. 70 odd years of companionship, friendship, and annoying behaviors - It all ends here at this memorial service. I designed it, the peach roses mixed with white calla lilies and bright orange tiger lilies surrounding a copper urn with a winding ivy pattern winding around, and around, and around it until every smooth surface inch is covered. I designed it for my life. I'm Bea, the eldest of three sisters whom I grew up defending and surviving with.

Ironically enough this is my urn, beautifully encased in hues of peach and orange, bright, bold but yet still subtle - just enough color to make people uncomfortable. They're my favorite colors all swirling around like ivy, around and around like my life's path, yet green and strong and nearly, impenetrable.

It's me they're remembering. This is my memorial. Beatrice was my given name, but I changed it as soon as I turned 16 to Bea. Beatrice sounds like a giant, old milk cow and I moved off the farm and into town. Bea is more me - gentle, caring, independent, loving and, well, now dead. I made it 84 years and if it weren't for the cancer I'd probably have lived a lot longer. Maybe.

They've all come to say "goodbye" and eat food, and complain about the too sweet peach wine. I was the oldest of the three "bad" eggs – the children that abandoned the farm for the city life and our own careers. I created my own career and eventually my own business in interior design. I can design! Despite what my Father always said. Our lives support the fact that girls don't HAVE to secure a husband, or if they did – it was by choice rather than necessity. I made my own way, thank you. I did end up marrying once, big mistake – but we'll get to that later. I want to give you my side of the story. I've made it to the pearly gates and am now looking down on the rest of you and them. But, I leave behind my two beloved sisters, Lois and Liz. They were the wild twins, who also left the farm but for the bright lights and beaches of southern California.

Those sluts never gained a pound since high school. Despite my prodding, they've never quit wearing mini-skirts and six inch heels either. Just picture it, you know you can: Two 80ish women, thin as pencils, not two muscles between them, wearing matching bright orange skirts with peach toned tops, Liz with a horizontal white stripe and Lois with a vertical brown stripe. It's only mid-October, not Halloween. I have to admit however, that they do add a dash of fall color to my flowers and copper ivy urn. Looking over the crowd while some unknown Pastor mumbles on about my family, I see the twins have missed putting hair coloring on a spot on the top of each of their heads.

Their frosted platinum blonde heads have a patch of gray right at the top. I've tried in vain to get them to stop frosting and teasing their hair in a swirling bouffant – it's so 1968 and it's 2014! Maybe it'll come back in style someday, but today is not that day. They aren't really twins you know. They just always like to dress alike and mimic each other's style. I'm 84, stocky, muscular and 5' 4" with natural gray-blonde hair. Maybe not exactly all natural, but close! Lois is a year older than Liz, and they just dress in the bright hues of the 1960's and keep their tall hair in a swirling stiff bouffant. Sometimes seeing them, I think for a moment that I've stumbled into a time warp.

Between them they have 226 pairs of shoes. All pumps, with at least 6-inch heels, nothing more, nothing less. Pointy toes and round toes, in a dazzling array of colors. Don't believe me? Check out their closets. Two women, one 4 bedroom house and 6 closets full of shoes and the clothes that match them all.

Neighbors, friends and our own family members insinuated or even stated they were weird. The harder Father tried to pry them apart, the tighter they clung to each other. They weren't weird in a homosexual kind of way, they were different and to most people anything different than their established norm, is weird. It's just the definition of weird. Eventually, it's the weirdness or proposed, rumored, whispered weirdness that drove all of us from the farm.

Drove us away from the family pressure to conform, the churches pressure to marry, and the overall female tendency at the time to go along with it all. Weird or not, we couldn't live with the female standard. We'll get to the family history reasons for all that in a bit.

I love this small town, or it was a small town when I was young. It's a fairly large city now in 2014, and growing in every direction but still agricultural at least on the edges. I hated the farm, hated the constant smell of dirt, fertilizer and sweat. I hated the endless days, the sticky insects, and the long, hot summers. It was always work, bugs, and dirt. Over and over again – work, bugs, sweat, and dirt. I was determined to move to town and get a job as soon as I turned 16. I saved what I could, scoured the store signs and names whenever Mother and I came to town to shop. She'd noticed me jotting down the names of the stores and the city streets.

When she'd asked why I was writing it down, the guilt swelled up inside me and in bursts and fits of sobs I managed to convey my wish to move to town and work for myself in a badly organized, tumbling mess of words. "Look at me," she said after a few minutes. I continued looking at my shoes. "Beatrice, look at me," she said again. Mother had 10 children and did nothing but work from dawn to dusk. She looked at me with her deep brown eyes, and said "Okay, but people will talk and your Father will not approve your leaving before marriage," she said in a warning tone. "It'll be much harder than the farm," she continued. "But, do what you must do, Beatrice. You're a bright, loving girl – and strong, you'll do fine. I will help when you're 16," she stated and off we went to the next store, not another word said.

Chapter 2

I did move into town the winter I turned 16, just after Christmas. Mother found the house, negotiated the rent and talked the local paint store owner into hiring me as a clerk. I was in heaven! For a woman who never talked much, she understood me perfectly well. I moved into a tiny, 800 square foot home right downtown – walking distance to everything! It had one bathroom, and two bedrooms and a small yard both front and back. It sat nestled between little homes just like it, no signs of a cow, a chicken, or a stalk of corn anywhere near it. I was thrilled.

Despite my personal happiness, a part of me always resented Lois & Liz moving to California. I worked two jobs to afford the little house downtown. I could walk to work, to the store, to the bank, and visit my newfound friends. They insisted it was awful. They wanted to see the ocean, sunbathe on the beach, and date movie stars! When I said it was too far, they argued it wasn't far enough. When I argued the cities in California were too big and dangerous, it only meant new and sexy to them. I was four years older and never been further from this town than Denver. I wasn't very fond of it, and I could not see how bigger cities in California could be better, but only worse. I'd lived in town two years when they both showed up at my door in matching autumn outfits, bags in hand.

They showed up on a Friday night three weeks after Mother passed away. They had everything they owned crammed into two bags, and a gunnysack. They couldn't stand it any longer. I took them in, of course. We squeezed into that tiny house and made up for lost time. They spent their spare time after school cutting out photos of the San Diego beach out of various magazines. They saved the little money they earned bagging groceries at the store and bought bikinis. They were determined. "You've made it, so can we," they'd argue as we sat together over dinner. When they turned 18 and 19, my "twins" left for California.

I took them to the train station and saw them off. When I dropped them off they looked like farm girls, white, slim, and each holding a small purse and two suitcases containing everything they had. They were equipped with a high school education, enough saved money to get them there, and a double dose of stubborn and independent. We'll check back in with them once they get to California. For now, let's get back to the present circumstances and my memorial.

I'm here looking over these people as they start rustling in their pew chairs, uncomfortable in the surroundings or just tired of sitting through another memorial. I'm thinking how long it's been since I've seen many of them, how much they've changed and how damn old they look! I see them commenting on the colors, on my choosing cremation. My fresh faced photo stares at them. Even with bad eyesight you can see that picture, loud and clear. I had it taken when I turned 30 and became the manager of the paint store. I had the glow of success and the full bloom of young adulthood.

Lois and Liz rose first to leave. Standing there in their bright orange hued outfits and matching patterns, they formed a solid contrast to those in less colorful outfits. Their bright heels clicked across the hardwood floor. Lois plucked my urn from amongst the flowers and then clicked her way down the aisle to the open front door. Liz stood at the entry and smiled, greeting everyone as they passed and pointing them downstairs for refreshments. Lois looked down, clinging to Liz's side, both hands on the urn. Their faces were worn and tired, but they had also a look of relief – it was finally over. As the last person made their way downstairs, they bolted (as fast as two old ladies in heels can bolt) down the front steps and out the doors of the church.

I followed, watching as they stowed me in the back seat of their Camaro and took off, convertible top down, and scarves billowing. Even the wind couldn't blow that hair though, only the scarves billowed past me in the urn. This is our story, our survival story – how we made it our way. It's our story of contrasts, colors, and the bright life – a life of outsiders. To understand us, our motivations to be "odd", or "not normal" you'll need a brief family history.

My parents immigrated to the United States from a German colony in Russia, just outside Odessa. They were farmers. Father was 21 and Mother 16 when they caught the train to escape Moscow and defect to the US. We never met our Grandfather, he died so we could live, my Father always said in a heavy, but nonchalant matter of fact way. After he'd had a few shots of bourbon in the evenings though, you'd get the whole horrid, bloody story – we were just never truly sure what to believe since when the bourbon was talking, some stories may have gotten exaggerated.

From Germany they traveled until they landed in New York and decided to head to Cheyenne, Wyoming where Father hand landed a job as a farmhand. Unable, after a few years, to find suitable farming land in Wyoming, they packed up and headed south to Greeley and purchased a 300 acre lot of dust and weeds. Father was well schooled and spoke fluent English. Mother only spoke Russian, so the three of us grew up speaking both. We had five older brothers and two older sisters or just enough hands to manage a small farm and a dairy. We all worked, sun up to sun down. Being the youngest, myself and the twins got assigned the smaller, but demeaning chores.

The boys worked in the fields or the barn. Mother started our mornings with a large breakfast complete with scrambled eggs, bacon, warm potatoes, and blinna or freshly sugared donuts. Leftovers we quickly packed into metal boxes and sent with the boys for lunch. Our older sisters trailed after Mother all day. We helped clean, and then the three of us set out to feed the hens and gather the eggs. After gathering, we washed each one and placed it in the icebox. Once that was completed, we'd have at least an hour or two to ourselves.

Hopping and skipping over clumps of dirt, we would end up at the small creek that ran about a quarter mile behind the house. One by one, in line, we'd step on stones and cross to the middle to stare at the muddy bottom and check for toads, tadpoles, or the occasional sand turtle. We were three children surrounded by open fields of corn, potatoes, hay, sugar beets, and sunflowers.

I would sit down on a nearby stump to rest, and watch the other two. Liz holds onto one of Lois's hands while she tries to stretch her arm and catch a tadpole that had just wandered into her view. Slowly she quieted her breathing, while Liz holding steady lets her lean further into the creek. She quickly snags a little toad in her open hand and Liz pulls her up. Gently, finger by finger Lois opens her hand and views her treasure. We pass the toad back and forth. "Time to get back," I say, "We have to start the wash." Lois puts the toad back near the bank, and we each slink back slowly towards the house. The washer sits just around the back corner of our house near the garage. It's a large white ceramic basin with a ringer in the center. I use both my arms and start the pump, up, down, up down until it's full. Then I measure out the exact amount of soap as Mother had shown me in previously, and grab the large ladle and stir. "Come on, you two are wasting time," I yelled as they slowly drug a cotton bag down the walk to the garage.

"Grumpy old cow!" Lois returns. Liz can't speak as she's out of breath. "It's heavy and it stinks!" Liz complains to no one in particular. The discussion continues until Mother comes around the corner to supervise. She gives us all a look and the talking ceases.

I throw the first few clothes in and spin them around. After a few rounds, Lois grabs each piece and starts it through the wringer. Liz then picks it up on the other side, and hangs them on the line, always on the seams and never in the middle she recites to herself. For Liz, the line always seemed a mile long. As the sun sinks below the distant mountains, I finally finish the last shirt. We're done! We head back to the house to bathe and get ready for dinner.

I'm responsible for drawing their bath. We each get 10 minutes in the tub so the boys have time to bathe while we make their dinner. Clean, cooled off and mostly refreshed we head downstairs to help Mother with the preparations. I'm responsible for setting the table with forks and spoons. Lois puts on the glasses, and Liz stacks the plates. We help Mother carry out dishes of mashed yams, cream gravy, ham, squash, butter and six loaves of warm, homemade bread.

Mother watches as each of us dig into the food, looking us over with a sense of gratification. Father bangs his glass against the table, and Mother jumps up to fill it with bourbon, again. At the end of the meal, Father announces that irrigating starts at dawn and everyone was to be at the barn. Silently, en masse we all quietly moan. Irrigating fields is a nasty chore.

At dawn we were all at the barn. We split up in groups, and head out. The three of us got the corn. We each took a turn moving the pipe into the ditch water, holding one hand against the open end as we whooshed the pipe through the water until suction made the water run. At the heat of noon, our brother Peter came to fetch us for lunch.

Our siblings and us shared a bond of surviving but we weren't close. They were closer in age, and we were 8 years behind them. Peter was our favorite brother because he always made sure we got our portion for lunch. He looked after us. Mother was always occupied, but kept a sharp eye on each while gathering each of us under her wing like a giant hen. Father was distant, a harsh taskmaster – it was his way of managing. He worked, ate and slept and had no use for talking. I never saw him hug any of us, mostly he just ignored the girls and worked the boys. When Father rose silently signaling the end of lunch, we all moved back to irrigating. In the early summer heat, I daydreamed of the day

I'd leave that farm. The day I'd finally be away from the dirt, the stench of sweat, and the endless variety of sticky bugs.

I dreamed of a husband, and a house surrounded by a lawn and flowers. Our house would sit next to other houses. The grocery store just steps away, and people would be shopping and talking to each other. Families with kids in tow mingling after working hours and playing games like it was Christmas day. It sounded so nice in my head.

I moved away at 16 with Mother's help. But, six months later, she passed away. Mother died in her sleep. Peter gave me the news over the phone the next day. The funeral was quickly put together since it was still harvest time. All the eyes were red except Fathers. He just stared straight ahead. He looked at me as if he didn't know who I was or didn't remember. He was drunk, which was typical. He sat present but not responsive. Peter eventually guided him out of the church and into the car, driving him back home. Two weeks later, he brought home Gracie, the stepmother. I still can't figure out to this day how he met a woman so quickly when he rarely ever left the farm except on market days and when he headed to town for liquor. From what I heard, she was a nightmare from day one. She cut Father off the bourbon, and took control of the family finances. Only Peter and Alex stayed, and our two older sisters were there just long enough to get married and leave. Home disappeared, although for me maybe it was easier because I was already gone. That's when Lois and Liz showed up at my door.

I earned enough at 18 to feed and clothe myself and pay the rent on my little tiny house downtown. I was in heaven! When Lois and Liz showed up at my door, they hadn't told anyone but Peter where they were going. So, I called home to let them know. I thought they'd be worried or had realized the twins had left. Father answered the phone. "Father, it's Bea," I stated. "Hmmm," he mouthed and passed the phone to Gracie. "We're not giving you any money," she stated. "You should be here helping your family with the farm not living in town like a commoner," she continued. Before she could get any further, I hurried and said "Lois and Liz are here with me." "Fine," she said and the phone went quiet. The conversation ended. "Peter," she yelled across the yard, it's Beatrice, or sorry, Bea." I could hear his heavy footsteps coming across the yard to the phone. "Hi kiddo," he quipped. "Lois and Liz are with me," I repeated. "I just wanted them to know they were safe." "I'll catch up with you at the market next week," he said. "Gotta go!" and he hung up.

I don't know what I expected. I headed back to the girls. They were unpacking and had already divided the extra bedroom into two equal halves. I left them unpacking and headed to the kitchen to see what I had to feed us all with. Our first night in our new lives we had fried eggs, potatoes and bread with strawberry jam. One of Mothers jam supply she'd left me last time she'd been in town.

"It's so quiet here, so peaceful. No yelling, no banging, and no chickens," Liz nearly yelled, a smile running from ear to ear. "Eggs straight from the store," Lois echoed. "And you can shower or bathe whenever you want, your own water too!" I added. Excited now, they headed to the shower. I resolved to wait until morning to shower as I knew it'd be a cold one if I used it tonight. Once they were asleep with their door open a crack I peeked in as one slept on the bed and the other on the floor. We concluded that we'd discuss further plans in the morning. We would sleep in and get up when we were hungry, whenever that was!

That time went by so fast for me. One day we were setting up twin beds and whatever matching accessories we could get, and the next day I was watching them wave discreetly from a train headed to San Diego. It seemed to me looking back, they were there just briefly and then gone again almost as abruptly as they'd come. They promised to call me when they'd arrived and then again when they'd found a place and settled in.

Chapter 3

The train rattled along, Liz and Lois took turns sleeping and watching over each other. They'd agreed not to fall asleep at the same time, so they could keep an eye on their bags and each other. They were both nervous and excited. They'd worked for two years to get the money saved for the train tickets, and a couple months worth of money they'd estimated for rent. They dreamed about the jobs they'd find, the city, the beach – mostly the beach, and the men they'd meet.

It was the fall of 1952, a time when women were just coming down from helping to fill jobs during World War II. As a group we were still riding the wave of independence brought on by a change in social history where women went to work. Many weren't willing to return the previous days where they were expected to quietly slink back into the shadows, marry, and have children. They wanted both or at least the option to choose.

Liz and Lois dreamed of time of beach parties, drinks, and nightlife the likes of which they could only imagine based off the photos in their magazines. It looked and smelled entirely different from the small farming community of Greeley. No longer would they smell fertilizer, wet dirt, or heavy sweat. They would be released from those small town ways where everyone watched and reported on everyone else. Instead, there would be, they imagined, at wild beach parties that started after 5pm and lasted all night long.

They'd already bought bikinis, and plenty of baby oil to get their tans started as soon as possible. They were heading to Monterey to a youth camp where they'd arranged a "temporary" stay through the church back home. They had 2 weeks to find jobs and a place to rent in Monterey. First they were going to spend two nights in San Diego and then take the bus up to Monterey. In the end, Liz and Lois stayed in Monterey for 30 years. They tanned at every beach from San Francisco south to San Diego and visited every coastal town in-between. Two weeks and three days later, they'd signed a rental contract on a little two-story house in Monterey just two blocks from the beach and stayed all weekend at the beach before starting their new jobs.

After unloading their suitcases and putting the final touches on her closet organization, Lois chimed "Let's go out tonight! There's that little bar off the coast just a half mile down the road, you know the one we passed on the bus advertising a beach party every night of the week?" "Are you sure?" Liz cautioned. "We need to be careful, you don't know what kind of men show up at beach parties." "The sexy Marlon Brando kind I hope," quipped Lois.

By 6:00 pm, both sets of hair were set and sprayed, and up high as the current style demanded. Make-up was on, perfumed and polished, they checked each other's outfits and found the matching pumps. Eager with anticipation and excitement over their first nightlife adventure, they set out down the sidewalk. They lived roughly two blocks from the beach and it was just a few short blocks down the beach to the bar.

Outside the bar were tiny lights outlining a small circle of sand, and a volleyball court. In the center to the left were several seats around an outdoor fire, embers glowing softly with the cool beach breeze. A small crowd had gathered around the few tables and chairs that were setup on a patio. It is a warm, almost clammy evening and the tables each had a small bowl of salted pretzels, peanuts, and a single pink calla lily in a vase.

Simple and tasteful, just their style! They circled around the patio, taking in the crowd and summing up the competition. They finally settled on a table just on the edge of the deck. Lois ordered red wine, and Liz a martini. They sipped their drinks and watched the crowd grow and swirl in circles. A young man approached them, looking very confident with his back straight and head up. He had a movie star gait as he glided down the patio, and casually without looking directly at either one of them asked if the other seat was available. "Yes," said Lois with a bold air, looking directly at him. Liz murmured quietly and sipped her martini. He didn't look trustworthy to her.

While this stranger settled in his chair, several other handsome, young men hovered nearby each scoping out the newcomers. A mixed group of youngsters then grabbed a volleyball from behind the bar, and managed to convince a few others to play a game. Laughing, drinking, and casually courting each other as they played. They laughed too hard at their mistakes while gracefully trying to ignore the mistakes of others. Liz and Lois were not the sporty type, they passed on each offer to play and remained tightly attached to their chairs. A few more hours, and a few more drinks later they'd loosened up enough to accept a few dances. They danced until the light of the sun was replaced by the gentle white glow of a full moon. Another game started, and they kicked off their pumps and joined in.

Liz was standing next to a tall man that looked like her favorite western actor, John Wayne, only much younger. He gave her a broad smile and stuck out his hand. "Toby at your service. What's your name?" Liz hesitated and looked around briefly for Lois, for support. Lois was already off in the back corner of the court chatting with the shifty eyed stranger from the table that Liz instantly hadn't liked. She smiled and answered, "Liz." "Glad to meet you Liz, whoops…looks like we're ready to get started," he answered and scampered into position. The men are both sides liked to encroach on her space but as the game went on and she deftly went left and right, backwards and forwards getting each ball, they finally backed off a bit. She might be tiny, but she was always quite competitive and could hold her own in sports even if she didn't enjoy playing. Toby grinned and shook his head at what he could recognize as a solid, stubborn resolve. Liz held her part of the court for a good hour.

Lois is far more reserved in her playing style. She doesn't mind at all, and always encourages the young men near her to go ahead and come over and help her out. A little bump here, a little bump there left her quite happy. Now, the men crossing her way were fine, but she wasn't very keen on any of the other young women crossing her way at all. She'd give them her icy cold stare and turn in the opposite direction. Lois lacked a bit of self-confidence as she felt she was not as elegantly pretty as Liz. Lois was more "cute" than "pretty." She always felt her nose was a bit long and thin, and she looked forward to the day when she could have it fixed! But, after awhile she'd get to chatting and laughing and forget about comparing her nose to anyone else's.

A few games later, they were really starting to tire. Liz caught Lois's eye and they moved to exit the game and return to the table. They'd both worked up a bit of a sweat and were feeling a bit warm, and possibly light headed from the alcohol and activity combination. Toby and Michael followed them back. Toby had his big brown eyes on Liz, and Michael had outmaneuvered the creepy young man Liz didn't trust. Michael was an aspiring actor who currently worked as a sales representative for a Pharmaceutical company. His territory included Monterey and most of the California and Oregon coast. Toby was a student at the local university and had a basketball scholarship. He worked a few hours on the weekends as a teller for his father's bank in town.

As the night went on and morning neared, they exchanged numbers and the twins walked the few blocks back home. They are both tired and suffering from a bit of a blush of alcohol mixed with some physical activity and active flirting. Flirting takes a bit more energy when you're starting out than anyone realizes. They were exhausted and quickly headed to their bedrooms to sleep.

Liz woke the next morning in a fog, listening to the phone ringing and ringing. Lois was nowhere in sight. She stumbled into the kitchen and finally got her hand on the phone. She glanced at the clock and it was 1pm! That can't be right, she thought to herself. I never sleep past 7am. "Hello," she chirped automatically and cheerfully on the phone. "Is Liz there?' Toby inquired. She instantly recognized the voice of the tall young man she'd danced with last night. Her muscles relaxed and she could still feel the warmth of his arms around her waist, the muscular strength of his body as he went after the volleyball. "This is she," she answered. "What are you doing tonight?" he asked. Before she could answer he continued, "There's a great seafood place about 10 miles towards San Diego, interested? I could pick you up or I can pick you both up if you'd prefer," he added. He finally paused, while Liz was working to stifle her immediate excitement and proceed with caution. She didn't know the man, but he seemed nice. But maybe that was going too far, too fast she worried. Maybe it'd be dangerous, but then again they could drive together and meet him there. As her mind raced, balancing the pros and cons, Lois's voice came on and she said, "Sure, we'd love to! Let me get a pen to write down the directions." She got directions, a time and they both said goodbye and hung up the phones. "It's quite a drive, and we don't really know him well," Liz said staring at Lois with her irritated expression. "And we'll never know if we don't try it, now will we," Lois countered. "He was a perfect gentleman last night, and maybe he has one for me!" she quipped, smiling and heading to the refrigerator. "I'm starving!" she announced.

They continued their discussion while they fixed their breakfast standard of one scrambled egg, two strips of bacon, and a slice of wheat toast. They made a plan to drive to the beach early and do some tanning, check out the area well before meeting for dinner. They also checked out the hotels just in case they stayed too late to drive back. Now energized they both started on their assigned household chores, evenly split in half. They re-divided it weekly because Liz still hated to do the laundry even though it was far easier now then it'd been when they were kids. Four hours later they had the house cleaned, and were dressed with hair high. They lightened a bit more than usual the past week, so it was a bit more blonde than they'd planned. However, they teased and pulled it around so it all swirled together and came off well blended. They decided to pick different colors of clothes this time so people wouldn't mistake them for twins. Lois chose red with a white top, and a blue scarf with matching navy pumps that included a tiny red bow on each buckle. Liz went with a bright yellow skirt, with a cotton yellow and white polka dot blouse that hung loosely around her hips. She picked matching white and yellow polka dot pumps with yellow heels. She was her own ray of sunshine.

They put their toiletries quickly together in a bag with a spare change of clothes, ended up using two bags to get everything they may need in case they decided to stay the night. As they drove, they stared at the flowers, the greenery, the sand, the ocean and the whole massive combination rolling together. Combined with the spring-like temperatures and the bright blue sky, it was perfect. Half way into their drive, they spotted a hamburger joint sitting at the far end of a public beach. They parked close, and found a spot and threw down their beach towels. They changed into their bikinis and laid down on the beach. They covered each other with baby oil and rolled like roasting chickens every 8 minutes. Maybe not like chicken, but rather like a browned apple pie. They napped, chatted, listened to the ocean waves wash by while they tried to relax. They were excited about their newfound freedom as well as what the evening may bring. They'd never eaten seafood, and hadn't been out much as yet since they moved into the house. Mostly they'd been occupied working and getting the house setup to suit their tastes. They'd bought a used car as well so their funds were rather depleted. Finally, they were out on the beach tanning, using their bikinis, and soaking up the sun! They agreed at that moment to call me, Bea, on Sunday and fill me in on what I was missing.

As the sun started to set in the afternoon, they shook out their towels and headed to the beach house to change. After all that work this morning, they had to redo most everything except their hair. It was still perfect. They showered, scented and got their makeup on in all the right places. They put on their outfits again, checked for sand and then headed back to the car. They packed their beachwear in the trunk and headed off to the restaurant. They pulled into the parking lot with 32 minutes to spare. Looking around they noticed that the restaurant hung partially off the cliff of the beach, so there were some significant stairs to climb. On the front side, a terraced garden flourished with thousands of white and purple calla lilies mixed in with tiny white baby's breath.

As they checked out the flowers, a Ford pickup truck pulled up close to them. Toby and another young man jumped out and waved. The twins took a long deep breath, and opened their car doors. "Great car, wow – where you work a bank?" Toby asked. "Yes," Liz quietly answered. "It's used she said, it only has a few thousand miles on it," she added almost guiltily. She didn't have to feel guilty, Liz said to herself. Lois gave both men a visual tour of the 1952 Pontiac Streamliner Coupe. Toby managed to remember his manners, and introduced them. "Liz, this is my older brother Thomas, or Tom for short," he said. "Hi, nice to meet you," Liz said. "And this is," Toby paused and Liz added "My younger sister Lois." Lois shook Tom's hand and Toby lead the way up the stairs to the restaurant door.

Chapter 4

The "twins" as I called them were always so polite, so polished. I was never sure where any of us got such a strong desire to be polite, done up, and perfectly polished. Perhaps it was part of what we didn't do growing up that made it more important to us as adults. Perhaps it was simply our way or acting like adults and being independent. We were free to be as clean and polished as we could afford to be. We will let the twins get settled into California and talk about me, Bea, and my life back in Greeley for a while.

The twins were working, getting out and meeting new friends, having new experiences, and had signed their own lease. That's a true event in our family. Of course it was their goal to be independent and meet eligible men, preferably Hollywood actors or sports stars, of course.

It was all the rage in our day – meeting eligible men. Your entire purpose it seemed was about just that. Meet a man and marry. Good gracious there were, and still are, reams of books written about dating, marriage, and raising children. It seemed like at the time that was life, is life and should be your life. For myself, I just wasn't into it. Maybe it was the "eligible" men weren't all that attractive, maybe it was because I was raised with brothers, or maybe it was just simply me. I was never interested in "eligible" men. No, now don't let your imagination run wild, I was plenty interested in men, just not necessarily the ones deemed "eligible."

I loved my comforts – earning my own living, and spending it as I wanted. Planning out my own future and dreams. Get that? My own future and my own dreams. The three of us before they'd left to California, talked for hours over coffee in the morning and then again with an evening glass of wine. We talked about our lives, our dreams, and how it would all turn out. Don't get me wrong, we weren't against men or marriage we all just wanted to run our own lives on our own terms, or as near as we could get to it.

Our brothers all married and were busy putting out children like puppies in the spring. One after another they'd come. We'd pool some money together and buy a nice gift. "When are you going to settle down," they'd ask. "When are you going to get married, met anyone yet," they'd say. "You're not getting any younger, you know. Kids are harder to raise when you're older," they'd continue on and on. Like they'd know – they were in their twenties and thirties – pure conjecture and assumption based on their own personal exhaustive state. When they continued with their line of questioning as I called it, my brain would take a time out. "Where did I see that cranberry pie recipe the other day? Which magazine was it? Oh, that's right, I have it on the counter where I was writing down the ingredients before I had to leave to get to a baby gift," I'd say mainly to myself.

Or I'd use the restroom break excuse: "Ah, time to powder my nose." I'd finally blurt out and head off to the restroom. It was the safest excuse there was and as adults, they wouldn't call you on it and therefore one could free one's self from questioning. Escaped again, I'd sigh as I bypassed the restroom and moved into the crowd hovering about the kitchen. It is the focal point of every home - the kitchen.

Eventually I'd find the hostess and politely thank them for the invite. Smile, then nod, and then wave while walking steadily, but not too quickly, to my car. You never want it to look like you're running. I'd get in, settle down into the roomy leather driver's seat and drive away, waving to no one as they'd all gone back to talking about their babies, and all the stories that come with that. The single girl was now gone. It was safe to talk again. "What does she do all day at work?" they'd ask each other. "I bet they don't work her very hard. Probably gets the coffee, wipes off the counter and takes out the trash." They'd chuckle amongst themselves, feeling better. They'd have to end by commenting on the "twins" move to California. "They aren't going to meet any good men out there. Not any better than we got right here." They'd say giving each other a salute with a beer. "It's all right here." The conversation always got worse before it got better which is why I always took off early. My brothers had one thing in common, they were all heavy drinkers and at some point in the evening an argument started. It kept them entertained because they never seemed to tire of talking, holding grudges, or arguing.

When I'd finally get back to my beloved little city home, the quiet and cleanliness would envelope me in a general feeling of peace. It was like a big, strong hug. It's one of the most beautiful feelings I've ever known – just pure, simple bliss. I'd slowly turn on the water and take a hot bath. Add a little lotion, a touch of perfume and some bubble bath and I'd be set. I'd drop my clothes into the nearby hamper and bury myself in the deep, hot water. "Ah, the beauty of living alone." I'd say to myself. "The beauty of not answering to anyone." Sometimes it took 15 minutes and sometimes I'd be in there for two hours it just depended on how the day had gone. My bath tonight would have to outlast the family party, so I'd surely be in here for at least an hour.

Finally as my skin curled, and my eyes started to droop I'd dry myself off and go straight to sleep. Other times, I'd think about the twins. Where they were and what they'd been up to. Maybe I should have gone with them? In living alone, I developed what I considered a normal habit of talking to myself. I'd carry on a full out discussion that covered politics, home life, what was right and wrong. I reviewed the latest styles of skirts and pondered the comfort and functionality of pants with flat heels versus skirts with high skinny pumps. I was on my feet more than half the day most of my life, so I generally opted for flat sandals or "slides" and comfortable pants. I never wore jeans, boots or work shoes once I left the farm. I didn't like dirt, sweat or the smell of either – and jeans or boots instantly brought back all those memories. Don't get me wrong, my memories were not all bad, but I just despised the smell of sweat and dirt both of which clung stubbornly to clothes worn for outside work. It simply was not me.

I wanted to be clean with a hint of perfume even when I did my yard work. I wanted to wear church clothes all the time. I wanted to wear jewelry and carry a beautiful handbag. I'm not really sure where that "need" developed from, but I think I just didn't want to appear to be a farmer's wife. I wanted to dress well, perhaps not as lavishly as my idol Elizabeth Taylor, but something close to that. You get the picture now. I was always clean, perfumed, and decorated with artfully matching jewelry no matter the occasion. I'd sew and hang draperies in the same dressy clothes. I dressed as well as I could. Over time, my fortunes fluctuated, but I always looked good.

The twins would tell you that we dressed to look "above" the farmers. We didn't want to be part of that group. We all wanted more of the dressy, country club styles ever so slightly above the working class even if the distinction was just in our minds. Thoughts do count in heaven – consider yourself warned. Just kidding! It's actually quite casual up here in heaven. Yes, I said heaven for those of you who didn't think I'd make it up here. Let's go catch up with the girls again and then I'll fill you in on my escapades.

Chapter 5

Earlier we talked about the world's obsession that women are supposed to search through the pool of "eligible" men and pick a husband. It was expected that a woman would marry, and in many ways still is. But in my prime, I was being constantly questioned by my brothers, and hounded by my father on why I hadn't yet married. Why wasn't I looking hard enough? Why did I want to end up being a spinster? You know, if wanting to make my own way in life made me a spinster, then one I would be – and I would enjoy it! I'd watched my mother eat after my father, and after her sons and then run herself ragged cleaning up after them.

When Mother died, our stepmother arrived to do the same thing. They gave up what to me seemed their entire lives, to fetch, clean and take care of their family. What about their life? Was it truly their goal, and purpose? What about romance, love, lust, or the full power of passion? What I'd seen of that growing up was sparse. Seemed to me, marriage was slavery. If you followed that path you were considered by many people a "good" woman. If you were like myself and my sisters, well, they had a variety of negative words for that. During my prime, or most of my working life, I enjoyed working with men. I admit I had a habit of falling for those all ready married. What made them so much more attractive? I think in my case, they seemed "safe." You could get to know them and become friends without any strings attached. I should have been able to relax, work with them and participate equally together. I was able to do that successfully at least 98% of the time. I just had trouble with that other 2%. One came along every so often that I just couldn't resist.

After working for the paint store and learning the tricks of the trade, I put all my money into opening a tiny little decorating store on my own. It was hard work, let me tell you but my former bosses helped me out. They were a married couple that ran the paint store together. She helped customers with decorating plans and he ran the financial and customer service side. They helped me get started and with all I'd learned from the both of them it was worth the extra effort. I finally had my own little decorating business in town – it was my dream coming true.

Back to the men in my life, like many women the one I truly loved also broke my heart. We had a good thing going for a few years. Let's start when he came into my shop as a salesman for a large home decorating and accessory supplier. He sold top of the line items, high quality, and exactly my style. The first time he stopped in and left me his card, I wasn't going to call him. He gushed over some photos of the last job I'd done and after I thought about it for several days,

I called Harry Lindshaw Perry back. I figured his line would enhance the variety of materials I could offer my clients. Harry showed up the next day and loaded up the store with his brightly colored items.

Maybe it was the way he looked at me. He didn't look through me or past me, but directly at me. I was used to being practically invisible. I got lost looking into his deep blue eyes. After that second meeting, I dreamed about him night after night until it started to get on my nerves. I imagined him leaning towards me, our eyes meeting, our lips briefly touching and then pulling away. That first gentle kiss turned into a harder, more forceful one as he wrapped his arms around my waist and pulled me into his arms. Clothes flew and we rolled together as one onto the couch in the storeroom, my heart pounding and his pulsing loins satisfying my every need. We would not emerge again until we were satisfied. As the moment passed, he held me tight in his arms. Of course, it could be I'd read too many romance novels. I dreamed about him for months, until he caught me in my daydreams.

Harry's hand touched my shoulder, "What are you up to?" he asked as I sat staring at my accounting sheets. He'd startled me because my mind was still on the pulsing loins part of my daydream. Caught in the act, my fair skin reddened, and my mind jolted back to the current time and place. He glanced around the store to be sure no one had yet wandered in as it was just past 10am, my opening time. Then he leaned to look right into my eyes and we kissed. Half of my mind screamed "No, no, no...he's married with several kids!" The other half of my mind took over with faulty human logic. I had suppressed my need for love and affection successfully for years, until now.

The kiss only lasted a few seconds, and then Harry finished unloading a few more boxes of new items and he dashed out of the store. "Call you later," he said smiling as he waved and sprinted to his car. He had several deliveries a day and apparently was behind schedule. At that point, I was still halfway between reality and my daydream. Once the door to the shop opened again and the chime sounded, I quickly gathered my thoughts to the present business need and went out to the shop ready to greet my first customer.

By lunch I had two more drapery jobs and had picked out two sets of matching towels, linens, and bedspreads for two homes. It was an active and productive morning. I typically had busy mornings and then slower evenings. I did most of my paperwork in the early morning before the shop opened and evenings after 3pm. In fact, my business grew so much in the first year I hired a young interior design student named Diana from the local university to watch the store in the afternoons so I could go out to client sites with Marvin, my drapery installer. I really enjoyed putting the finishing touches on a client's install and insuring everything looked as good together in the final product as it had in my mind. It was exhilarating to see it all fall into place, whether I'd done an entire house or just a single room. It was pure joy to me to see what I'd envisioned become real.

My customers were pleased, at least most of the time. Every so often our final visions didn't coincide and Marvin and I took it all back to the shop to make adjustments. It was just part of the business. Before computer animation and graphics, we sketched out patterns and ideas on paper. Most of the time the idea came across clearly, but now and again they didn't. One time my rendition of a pink and peach poppy on a cream base didn't translate as expected. We'd try again and eventually end up on the same page. Re-dos were popular items in the shops clearance bin.

A few days after "the kiss," Harry called.. Harry Perry – can you imagine! But, he was a charming man in his early thirties. I'd dated a few young men during my late teens to early 20's but had never found anyone so compelling. Admittedly, I was focused on my career and when I'd gotten my own shop I was even more so. All my hard work was on the line – it represented who I was and all my years of work, money, and labor. Yes, we all have a need for love and affection – the human mating dance. But my past encounters never left me with much except feelings of regret and anger. Harry was different. He had an infectious good humor, was tall and relatively handsome. His huge smile and bright blue eyes covered any other visible flaws that I could see. He sold decorative items from exotic places like New York and Chicago, items difficult to get in Greeley. Harry had good taste, and our styles were quite similar.

Ultimately, I fell for him because he had a way of looking directly at me while he talked. Harry didn't look through me as if I wasn't there, nor did he ever look past me as if waiting for someone else to appear. Nope, he looked directly at me and I'd get lost in the depths of his blue eyes. I'd look at him, and then shake my head to bring myself back to the business deal we were discussing or reviewing the items I wanted to purchase. As we worked together more frequently, he'd show up close to lunch or dinner. Naturally, we'd go for a short break at either lunch or dinner, but as our friendship progressed it seemed we did more dinners than lunches. To be honest, lunch was easier on my schedule, but to spend time with Harry was high on my list. He made me feel warm, smart and loved. I suppose it was inevitable, we moved from a business relationship to a friendship, and then to a love affair – mixing business and pleasure. A volatile mix for sure, but it worked for both of us for two short years.

Apart from the end, it was one of the happiest times of my life and likely the best relationship I ever had. Harry treated me with more respect and genuine affection than anyone in my life. Although my family was horrified because of the affair, I continued on. Even before they'd realized he was already married, several of my brothers had actually told me he was homosexual, because he was too sensitive. He listened too much. I fell head over heels in love with Harry despite their disgust.

About a year into our affair, Harry announced to me one evening after dinner that he was going to leave his wife and move in with me. Part of me was happy, thinking of the possibility of spending so much time with each other. However, another part of me was quite happy with our relationship as it was. To this day, even in death – I think I preferred just being in a relationship with my best friend. We'd have been better off. But, as you can likely imagine, his wife and the farming community in which we lived and worked disapproved.

To be honest, humanity may be a happier, gentler place without being tied and bound to each other. In a way, it would really improve human relationships overall or at least that philosophy sounded good to me at the time. But, I squashed those feelings and Harry moved in. We remained close friends and the intimacy was fantastic. After a few months, Harry started to change, or perhaps not really change but I discovered a side of him that I did not like. It was a side that reminded me of my father. It's hard to describe, it's a coldness, a distance, that arises in a relationship. It's not adversarial exactly, but it's not loving either. It's almost like an assumption of control, mixed with a need to protect added to a need to impose rules and instill them with a threat. I wouldn't go so far to say, it was violent in our case, but it had that subtle hint of domination. Perhaps like one may feel as a woman during sex, sometimes based on the inherent nature of the act, men are dominant or feel like they've conquered a dragon or won a war – or who knows what goes on in their heads. All the candles, sexy lingerie, and perfume can't cover it up, neither can diamonds, gold or money.

For myself it was both frightening and exciting, but ultimately inspired me to want to take a steak knife and stab it repeatedly in his chest. Although the feeling went away, thank goodness for me, it was still disturbing. I could visually imagine killing this man at the same time wanting to make love to him – but that moment of depression, of sadness, of feeling under control I certainly hated. Harry never knew why I'd slip away afterwards for a cup of coffee and spend time away from him until I could get my mind back to a saner side of normalcy.

It all started with Harry started watching my every move. He made nasty comments about customers and generally became an overbearing, domineering, jealous, giant pain in the ass. For example, he'd drive by to see if my car was at the shop in the morning and then again at lunch. Any time I looked at another man, or talked to another man he'd accuse me of cheating on him. Harry's accusations happened almost every night of the week because I talked to a lot of men. He even accused me of having an affair with Marvin and it was when he threatened Marvin that I knew he had to go. Fortunately for me, it was easier than I thought. Harry stormed into the store one morning and announced to the world he was going back to his wife. I loved him and I still do, but I was so grateful that his wife took him back and they moved across the country.

Oh, my business took a small hit, my reputation in town got a bit muddied. People looked at me with disdain and often whispered behind my back as I passed. But, after he left, the clouds eventually lifted and the sun rose again. Even now, I'm glad Harry and I had a relationship and I'm glad it ended. Business boomed and I was doing well. I Found another carpet and accessories salesperson, a few actually. They all looked directly at me and many are here today at my memorial, good friends but never lovers. Ah, losing Harry's affection hurt for a long time, but all things considered it was worth it. I loved, laughed, cried and in the end regained my self again.

It was all rolling along just fine until I got the call that Sunday from a sheriff in Monterey, California. It took me a few seconds to understand why he was calling. Liz had been seriously injured in a car accident. I left the store in the hands of Marvin my drapery hanger and Diana my student assistant and headed to California by plane. I'd never flown before and despite my initial reservations, I would have enjoyed the trip if I hadn't been worried about Liz.

Chapter 6

Let's catch up with the girls on their first date in California and put my troubles aside for a moment.

As the foursome reached the top of stairs of the restaurant, they could smell beach mixed with grilled steak and garlic. It was a gentle, not too pungent odor that drifted lazily from the kitchen to the front door. The interior was fairly dark, with small lamps on each table and a subtle golden glow from above. As they looked around, their eyes adjusting from the afternoon sun, on one side was a cozy room decorated in warm reds and sporting a fireplace. On the other side sat a huge bay window that encompassed several tables and a panoramic view of the ocean. That room had the expected nautical seashell theme and glowed sea-blue.

A youngish woman of around 40 popped her head through the double kitchen doors with a welcoming smile. "I'll be with you all in one minute," she said. Right on time she popped through the double doors again, grabbed four menus from the hostess stand and turned to the four. "You all are here early, you've beat the crowd. Do you want the ocean view room or the warm room," she asked. "Ocean, please," they responded almost at once. "Ocean it is," she said and walked them to a spacious square table directly in the middle of the window. "Anything to drink?" she asked. "Or do you want a few minutes to check out the menu first?" "We have a variety of wines and beer available as well. Check it out and I'll be back in a few minutes," she said. She gave them all a quick wink as she spun around and headed back to the kitchen.

They sat separated on either side – ladies are on the left and gentlemen on the right. Each group had a good view of the water, including even some of the beach. For a few minutes they all sat and watched the water. Toby broke the silence by noting to the girls when the tide was moving out. He pointed out the rocks with a white line that marked the point of the tide. They couldn't see the details, but it made for a nice starting point for conversation. Lois chuckled to herself and then pointed out a pair who were chasing their beach chairs and picnic items and trying to retrieve them from the water. Tom sensed an opening and asked Lois where they'd come from, if they were students or worked – the usual awkward chatter of those on a first date. Lois and Liz took turns giving a brief overview of the family and farm in Greeley, leaving out details about the personal conflicts with the lifestyle. Neither wanted to appear ungrateful to their parents. They painted a pleasant picture of a large family including several brothers and a wicked stepmother. Liz added in that ever since grade school they'd planned to go to California after seeing pictures of the trees and ocean in a US History class.

Liz wanted to see the ocean, the birds, the flowers and the year around pleasant weather. She blushed as she described how they'd often play as if they lived in a palace where the back yard sat right against the ocean. Dolphins would swim up to the deck and wait to be fed. Sea gulls built houses along the deck, and kept everything squeaky clean. Lois rolled her eyes – wondering why Liz picked such a childish and boring story. She finally got Liz to stop when their drinks arrived. Toby took the opportunity to order two appetizers for them to share and while they sat in the slightly awkward silence again, they each read their menu, oohing and aahing over the wide variety. Toby decided on a steak and shrimp combo, Tom went for the salmon and both ladies got the fish and chips. Liz and Lois weren't sure what to order. The only thing they'd really tried so far was clams and lobster. They hadn't been all that impressed with either one. Neither wanted to admit they knew nothing about seafood.

Tom pitched in for a bottle of red wine for them while getting himself a beer. Toby pointed out the local favorite. Lois really preferred white wine, but at this point, she was hungry and thirsty and not picky. After all, free wine was still wine. They finished discussing their jobs, family histories and then their food arrived. Between the wine and the conversation, Liz was exhausted, her eyes starting to close every so often. Fortunately, they'd arrived before the main crowd. They'd been there an hour, enjoying their meal and the people kept filing in, until nearly every single table was full.

The conversation moved like a roller coaster at a theme park. They'd get talking, eat a bit and then stall for a few minutes as if they'd lost the thread of the conversation. Up, down and then around they'd go. Toby was the dominant leader, and tended to keep the conversation going. He didn't much care for silence, so any lags in the conversation of more than ten minutes or so would cause him to think of another topic to start the group on. They moved from personal topics to the more general. Lois & Liz being new to the area compared the general seasonal patterns between Colorado and California.

Just when Liz thought she may drop off to sleep completely, Toby would smile her way and ask another question or perhaps not a question, but some effort to keep the conversation going. Finally, he landed on local sports and that topic kept them all rolling along through the rest of the meal. High school football, baseball, basketball – Toby actually knew a few professionals in baseball. Football wasn't at that time nearly the huge crowd pleaser it would later become. In my older years I watched the NFL every single Sunday. I knew there was one thing I'd miss being dead.

At the end of the meal, the girls knew about the radio and TV stations that carried the local college and professional baseball games, even though they didn't necessarily care. Lois & Liz had a habit of "exchanging glances: to signal each other, a sort of conversation as it were. Right at this particular moment, Liz was signaling, she was tired and ready to head back. Maybe it was the sun bathing earlier, or the walking along the beach, or just having the day off, but she was exhausted. As she glanced at Lois, while Toby and Tom went down another "compare our skills at sports" conversational exchange, Lois glanced back to say "let's finish this up and go." First, they demurely turned down dessert, and refrained from any further drinks. When they reached an impasse, or a significant lull in the conversation Lois looked pointedly at her watch and said, "I've had such an enjoyable evening, but we need to get back. We've had a full day." "Are you sure?" Toby asked. "There's still time to take a stroll on the beach, check out the evening tide," he said mostly to Liz. Tom asked if they were splitting up in different cars – or taking the same one. Lois stared him down for a few seconds until he said, "So, you all are heading back home together then?" "Yes, " said Lois. She didn't want to totally discourage him, so she added "How about hanging out at the beach tomorrow morning?" "Say, about 10am? We can check out the boardwalk," Liz added. "Let's meet at the main beach tomorrow and take in some scenery," she said.

Although scenery wasn't exactly what Tom was hoping for, he figured it meant he still had possibilities. Toby waved down the waitress for the bill and he and Tom split it. Liz insisted on leaving the tip, at minimum, if not money for the drinks. Toby stubbornly declined – there was no way a woman was going to pay on his date. He didn't care how independent they were. He finally agreed they could leave a tip. Still playing the gentlemen, they waited for the ladies giving them a hand up from their chairs and then offering the crook of an elbow as they descended the long stairs to the parking lot. They walked the ladies to their car and finished making Sunday plans. Toby and Tom had to be back at work by 6am Monday, and Liz & Lois by 9am.. It still gave them part of the morning to check out the boardwalk and then spend time at the beach before they all had to head home to Monterey.

Liz piped up and offered to bring sandwiches and a picnic lunch. Lois, somewhat surprised by Liz's offer, agreed. Toby closed the car door once Liz was settled inside. Leaning through the window, he gave her a quick kiss on the cheek. She blushed and he beamed with pride and wandered off to his car, Tom following behind. Lois kept her window up and only waved. For her, he'd have to do quite a bit more than just dinner before he'd get even that far with her, thank you very much.

After the men had gone, Liz pulled out onto the road with Lois chiding her about the picnic food. "Let's find a motel nearby and stay for the night and ddrive home tomorrow," Liz said. "Love to," Lois answered but you promised to bring picnic food. Where the heck are we going to find a store?" she asked. "We'll find one somewhere," Liz said. "I'm certain someone at the motel will know – or can point us to a local store, " she said. "The evening was nice, but I didn't want them to get the wrong idea," she added. "I like Toby." "He's way too bossy, "Lois said. "He thinks he's the one we should be doting on. He talked about himself most of the night. Except when it reminded him about his lack of baseball skills," she said. "I think Tom really likes you," Liz said changing the subject. "We'll see how tomorrow goes when there's no wine or food to distract us," she said smiling. Liz pulled into the motel and they went in and got a room. They parked in front of their door and headed inside.

The room was warm and smelled like Pine Sol, but it was clean and welcoming. They took turns cleaning up for bed and changing into their pajamas. "So, what do you think of Toby, really?" Liz asked. Lois rolled her eyes at no one. "Let's see what tomorrow brings. He just seems bossy to me, like Father." "But, I'll have to say dinner was nice, I did enjoy the food," she said. "What did you think about Tom?" Liz quizzed. "He's cute, but quiet," Lois answered. "He seemed to feel out of place, like a bull eating off linens," she said. Liz fell asleep dreaming of Toby. Seeing him playing baseball, sweating, and running bases while the sun glistened off his brown, slightly curly hair under his cap. Toby had large arms, slightly chunky but not fat. He had an Italian look, with brown hair and was around 6' 2". He was kind, authoritative but not overly pushy. Liz thought his manners were above average, or at least above what her brother's were. As she drifted off to sleep, she imagined them walking hand in hand down the beach, bare footed in the sand. She drifted off to a peaceful sleep. Lois laid awake watching Liz, smiling and grinning. She only imagined what she was thinking.

Lois shook her head in dismay. Liz was a romantic, Lois a realist. Love like Liz dreamed of, Lois was convinced didn't exist. She herself had never seen it. Not in her brothers relationships, and certainly not in her parents. Relationships seemed to Lois to be more about utility, like business. Their point was survival, children, and male support. For Lois, it seemed that women did a lot of work in support of their brothers, then their husbands, and then their sons. It seemed more like servitude. Life as a woman knew it was dependent on the whim of a man. True, a couple of her brothers seemed to truly adore their wives – but even that wasn't great odds. To Lois, most women were servants and she vowed quietly to herself that she and Liz would not suffer that fate. As much as Lois loved me (Bea), she considered me weak and figured I'd give up and marry, just to get a nicer home near the Greeley Country Club. I knew what she thought of me, but I ignored it.

Lois promised herself and Liz that night, that no matter what, they'd be strong, independent women who made their own way through life and used men rather than being used by men. She too, drifted off to a contented sleep, smiling despite the itchy curlers that clung to her hair and grated against her scalp – all for the sake of a head of full, curly hair for a morning date with a man she wouldn't even consider marrying. For the record, it was years before I "gave up" and I truly loved the man I married.

Chapter 7

As the plane landed in the foreign state of California, I started to wonder if the accident was real or an excuse to get me out to do something for them. I planned to visit, but not at this time. However, in retrospect is there really ever a good time to take time off from work? When you have your own business it's risky to leave it in other people's hands. As I entered the airport, I saw the tiny figure of a very pale Lois leaning against the far wall adjacent to the restroom looking impatient. Dark sunglasses that took up much of her face, bright blonde hair swirled on top, and a dark navy mini-skirt. Her face appeared rather stern, but curled up into a half-hearted smile when I approached.

"Finally," she said. "Glad you made it. I was afraid you'd be circling around for another hour," she added. "How is Liz?" I asked. I hadn't gotten more information than she was in the ICU, expected to live but would need help for a few weeks. I also didn't know what had actually happened and was hoping to get more information out of Lois. "She's okay. Mostly bruised and sore, with a bruised lung and a broken leg," she said. She elaborated a bit as we got my bag and then walked to the car and drove the ten minutes to the hospital. I noticed that everything seemed so close here. Nothing was more than ten minutes from their home. It was a wonder they bothered with a car at all, I thought to myself. But as we all know, cars are not so much a necessity but rather a show of success – a trinket that was hard to miss and a distinct signal that one is doing well.

As we made our way through the hospital halls, Lois led the way directly to Liz's room. It was mid-morning and just after breakfast, so she was sitting propped up and looking out the window. The only view was of a courtyard and the next building over. However, there were a couple of trees, one with a small bird feeder attracting a lot of attention from a variety of colorful birds.

She smiled at me as Lois and I entered the room. It was a weak smile, but it was a welcoming one at the same time. My heart gave a sigh of relief because at least she looked like she'd recover. She recognized me and seemed mostly alert, in pain for sure, but as alert as medications allowed. Doing the math quickly in my mind, it'd been just over a year since we'd seen each other in person. Granted, we talked on the phone weekly but it was so good for me to see them both in person, even if it was not in the most pleasant of circumstances. We went through the usual general pleasantries including a light hug and a kiss on top of her head. She was my baby sister after all.

We talked a few minutes about my life including changes in the store, how I was doing – any men in my life and all that sort of thing. After we got through it, she got tired and drifted off to sleep. The nurses came in and out, checking and re-checking, noting her vitals and updating her chart. Her doctor stopped in as well, and I got the unabridged version with all the details that Lois, still down the hall, had left out. It was a lot of information to sort out.

Liz had sustained a broken fibula on her left side, as well as 3 cracked ribs and a punctured lung. He expected to keep her in the hospital for at least 5 days and maybe more depending on the lung. I understood most of what he'd said, but not quite all.

During my conversation with the doctor, Lois slid quietly into the corner chair. Once the doctor left she stood suddenly and announced she was going down the hall for coffee. "Would you like some coffee?" she asked, looking at me. I headed out the door with her. "Toby is already out," she said with little or no emotion. "Was he hurt at all?" I asked. "Yes, but not seriously. I think he just broke his right arm and collar bone," she said flatly. "Do you know what happened?" I asked. Right then, we turned the corner into a small cafeteria where she walked up to the counter and ordered two black coffees. As we headed back with our cups, she sighed and said "He drove off the side of the road, never even tried to stop it seems, may have been a bad brake cable. It's hard to say really. I imagine he didn't take very good care of his truck," she added. "Hmmm," I said and nodded watching her reaction. "When we talked on the phone, she seemed to really like him. She was getting serious about him I'd thought," I added. It'd been a week and perhaps a couple days since I'd last talked to Liz on the phone, but she'd been very upbeat and excited both about her job and Toby. It seemed like she thought she'd found another man who was "the one." I mention it because in high school Liz dated a boy named Robert Gaines for nearly three years. He'd been a local football hero, clean cut and quite popular. It was expected they'd be married when Liz graduated but it was not meant to be. Robert had been killed in a traffic accident, swerved and hit a farm truck in the middle of the afternoon driving home for the weekend from Ft. Collins where he'd started college.

Fortunately, the truck driver was not injured. The local police came around asking questions at the house for a month or two before they'd agreed the accident had been just that – an accident. Apparently, there'd been some question on whether the car's brake lines had been partially cut or sliced. However, they'd never found any evidence and so they chalked it up to tragedy.

I sipped my coffee and sighed. "Do you remember Robert? Poor Liz she was so crushed when he'd died," I said. "Yeah, I remember him." Lois answered. "He was not a nice guy, he got what he deserved," she said. "What? He wasn't mean to her that I remember. Not at all," I said disturbed. Memories of our high school years flickered through my mind like a slide show at high speed. True, I was out on my own when Lois and Liz went to high school but I saw them nearly every day. Liz had gotten engaged to Robert her senior year. He was two years older and worked for his father selling Pontiacs while he attended college. His family owned the first Pontiac and Chevrolet auto dealer in town. I remembered spending nearly that entire summer helping Liz plan her wedding. She spent every available moment she could with him, even if it was just hanging out at home with her brothers and father all watching him from the corner of their eyes. "As I recall, that's one of the only times you two spent time apart," I said, remembering how angry and annoyed Lois had been. She'd refused to do any wedding chores, no matter how simple. She was just simply angry all summer, slamming doors and not talking to anyone. We all shrugged it off as something she'd get over once Liz was married and gone.

"What did he do? I surely don't remember anything bad," I said. As she spoke she stared at the floor. She never looked me in the eye when she was lying, and as the older sister I'd used this when watching over them. What was she not telling me? What had she experienced or heard about or seen? I'd no idea. Alarms were going off in my head, you know the kind that keeps telling you something you don't really want to hear, but it won't stop talking. "She's better off now than she would have been had she married that creep," she said. As I remembered, it was Lois who'd coaxed

Liz out of her gloom and depression and back into their dream of moving to California. Liz had entertained herself by drawing pictures of how she dreamed it would be. Lois had also gotten them both jobs together at the diner just outside of town so they could save money for California.

They'd moved in shortly thereafter with me when our Father had remarried. My thoughts turned to what Lois had done when Liz was spending all her time with Robert. She'd occupied her time helping her brother's fix tractors and farm trucks. She'd been small enough to squeeze into tight spaces and her hands were so much smaller, she'd found it easier to access some parts. Her brothers enjoyed showing her what was what. She'd actually developed quite a knack for fixing engines. I stared at her for a moment. Thinking, she wouldn't have, couldn't have, no, no, surely not. "What?" she asked as I stared at her contemplating just how far she'd go. "Oh nothing," I said quickly, "Just thinking back." "Let's spend some more time with her tonight and then I'll take you to our place," Lois said.

"We can make a plan for the week and have a bite to eat," she added. I shook my head to clear the dark thoughts running through. It's not possible, I said to myself.

We stayed with Liz for another couple of hours and then we shuffled out the door for the night as visiting hours ended. Lois handed me the keys and she gave me directions. Lois never liked driving. Liz did all the driving. A short ten minutes later we arrived at their home. They had a small balcony on the second floor and a tiny concrete patio in the backyard. It was a Spanish stucco style over-run with flowering vines. It sat two blocks from the beach, and about 10 minutes from the main shopping area, medical offices and the business offices. They had sublet for a low rate from a professor going on a long term sabbatical overseas I learned from Lois.

Inside they'd decorated in largely gold and avocado green, subtle and modern for the time. Two stuffed chairs sat circled in front of a small TV with a radio on top. They'd gathered seashells, cleaned them and put them into jars and spaced them throughout. They had a small kitchen, and a decent sized bedroom each. The top floor held the bedrooms and a full bath. The lower floor had the kitchen, a small den and a backyard patio. The lawn was bright green and a surprisingly large. The fence was crawling with blooming vines in yellow, pink, and red blossoms. Liz had planted a small garden patch. Lois picked 2-3 tomatoes while showing me the backyard. There were two tomatoes, two cucumber plants, and one zucchini. It was plenty to provide the two of them with some exercise and a few vegetables. Of course, they could just buy fresh vegetables on nearly every corner, but it was a nice connection to home on a small scale. I knew they missed Greeley even if they'd never admit it.

I was quite tired, especially after I knew Liz would be okay. "Would you like some wine?" Lois asked. "No," I answered. "I think I'd just like to get cleaned up and go to bed. I'm exhausted." "You can stay on the couch or Liz's room , up to you," she said as she poured herself a large glass of white wine. By the time I made it up the stairs with my bag to Liz's room, she'd already downed one glass and was pouring herself another. Probably just nerves, I told myself. She's had a hard week, I told myself and turned my focus to a hot bath, my clean pajamas, and sleeping. We'd always been raised to wake up early and get to work. So, as usual I woke up at 5 a.m. and got myself dressed. I made my way downstairs and started the coffee percolator. As it's smell drifted through the house, I dug around the fridge and found some bacon and a few eggs. I cooked up both and put two slices of bacon to the side to smuggle into Liz. I then stepped outside the front door and grabbed the local paper from the front porch.

I read through the headlines, and the political columnists, and then I checked the weather. There were numerous stories about local actors and actresses, mostly interviews or short personal background stories. Sitting there quietly reading the news reminded me that I hadn't called Peter, my brother, before I'd left. I typically called him every Sunday morning before he and his family headed off to church. We'd catch up on the family news – it was my personal version of the Farm Report. The farm was running quite successfully. Peter and Roger had gotten together and purchased a second farm roughly twenty minutes away that had two homes, so each family had their own space. It gave the two still at home more room as well. Our older brother, Isaac had disappeared it seemed. They weren't sure where he'd gone, but he'd taken up with a 15 year old girl (Isaac was 30) recently and they'd both disappeared. Isaac had always taken Father's incessant prodding to heart. He was a fiery, quick-tempered and stubborn man that shared Father's love of bourbon.

Father found out about Isaac's young girlfriend from the butcher in town with whom he regularly shared breakfast with before setting out on the day's chores. He'd thrown Isaac out that night, and called the police. Father made it clear no one still at home was to help Isaac but that didn't include me since I'd already left home. We would have helped, just so we would know what happened to him. Even if we'd not been that close to him, he was still our brother and we never did know how he'd fared as life went on. Admittedly, I know now, since we're both up here looking down. But that's another story for another time.

After I caught up with Peter, I called Marvin to check up on my store. All was well, so far, so good. I sighed to myself, and sipped my coffee. Seems all was well without me. I jotted down a note to leave Lois some cash to pay for my long distance phone calls. I didn't realize she'd walked in until I'd hung up the phone and started digging around in my wallet for cash. "Is any of this for me?" She asked as she glanced over the bacon and eggs. "Of course, " I answered. "I just pulled out a few pieces of bacon to take to Liz. I know how she loves bacon." "It'll give her a nice taste of home." I added. "This is delicious, thank you." Lois said as she chowed down. Visiting hours started at 10am, so we spent a few minutes making a plan for the day. I'll tell you, we sure got our exercise walking back and forth from the hospital, to the grocery store, and then to some shops down along the beach.

While I was there, we caught a bus to the new "mall" they called it about an hour away. It was a magnificent site – especially to those who love, new and shiny items. It was a cluster of stores, all inside one connected building. It included several fountains and benches to sit and relax on as you made your way from store to store. Lois and I found two chairs and matching lamps that would add some color to their décor. We also found a couple of huge paintings to brighten up their walls. During that week, Lois continued to go to work and I repainted their entire apartment. I got it finished one day before Liz returned home. Liz returned to a slightly brighter room, and a few more decorative pieces. She smiled when she saw it, so I'm thinking she liked it. I'd worked hard to tone it down a bit, because I knew she liked more subtle color tones. At any rate, she had a comfortable chair, a new light and a clean place when she came home. I then returned home to Greeley exhausted, never remembering about Toby's car until several months later. In the meantime, Liz recovered and was warmly welcomed back at the bank. Life went on again, quietly, at least for a while.

We all know after all, that life is like a roller coaster where the seats are a bit tight and the bars holding you sometimes loose. Up, down, slow, then fast with wicked turns, slow climbing hills and hideously quick and often sudden descents.

Chapter 8

Before heading back to Greeley, the three of us made a pact that every year we'd take turns visiting each other for at least a few days. There were two options, meeting at home or meeting at another location. Personally, I wanted to see Rome, New York, and Chicago.

I didn't think any of those plans would come true, but I was still working on them all. The first couple of years we simply visited back and forth. I even arranged a family reunion in Greeley at my store after hours. Although tastefully decorated by myself and catered by a local restaurant, the best part of the entire ordeal was how wonderful the store looked. The turnout was good. Peter took a break from his farm and came in with his wife Evelyn and their four kids. Roger brought his family but left after 15 minutes when an argument over weed treatment chemicals turned ugly. Lois broke up that fight. Of the five brothers, three showed. Brian and his group I finally had to send home, with packaged leftovers, nearly three hours after everyone else had left. Father and Gracie made an appearance. They sat stiffly side by side on the sofa next to Peter most of the evening. I filled them in on Liz's recovery, what California was like, and our vacation pact. I know they saw my mouth moving and I know it made sense because Peter understood, but they never responded.

Peter took them home after a few hours and returned. I think I saw them eat, but I'm not certain. The three of us girls enjoyed spending the evening mostly with our two older sisters. We discovered that Marian and her family were planning to move to Portland, OR. Justin her husband, had gotten a work promotion. She believed the trees would be beautiful. Eunice changed her name to Tea and after divorcing her first husband the previous year and was set to be remarried in two months to an actor she met during a stop he made in Windsor. None of us could fathom how that could have happened. No cultural events ever stopped in Greeley at the time, and certainly not Windsor. Eunice (now Tea) had always been known to fabricate wild stories. None of us had seen this New York actor man, so we probably looked doubtful. Believe her or not, she was set to move to New York in two weeks.

It was great to catch up, so despite the boys fighting and our wordless Father, overall it was a success. I'd almost made it to the finish line when Tea and Lois started screaming, each one with a solid hold on the others hair. Lois's hair proved to be a bit stiff for Tea's grip, so when she let go, Lois whipped her around until she rumbled to a stop. Then, Lois jumped on top and started whaling on Tea with both fists. Tea was crying and it all ended with Tea biting Lois in the arm. Peter finally got them separated and I tried to keep Lois at bay. After the tears were cried out the hair put back in place, Tea left to get home before her man called. Peter pulled the cause of the fight out of Lois. Tea had accused her of killing Robert Gaines and ruining Liz's chance of finding true love and marriage. The accusation was a repeat and as usual was quickly followed by a rather guttural exchange of expletives and name-calling. Liz dismissed the accusation with a rolling of her eyes. "Tea has a vivid imagination," she said.

As Liz, Lois, and I finally sent the last group home, Lois poured us each a glass of white wine. "Dear God, that was painful," she said. "Let's not ever do that again." "At least we got to see each other, with a few exceptions of course, " I said. "All in all it was a success," I said as I sipped my wine. A real vacation would be more relaxing I thought to myself as I watched us each relax until Diana my assistant showed up to help clean. Lois and Liz helped reorganize items that had been rearranged while I vacuumed and Diana dusted. After a few quick hours, the store was put back together and ready for Monday morning. The girls stayed with me a few more days and then headed back to California.

The next year went fast. I worked overtime with Marvin getting draperies hung and spent more time with Diana so she'd better understand the business aspect of interior design. Between drawing out sketches of my plans, finding the right fabrics, and locating reasonably priced matching decorative accessories, I didn't find myself with much time for anything else. Once I got the design work done then I had to keep up on the bookkeeping as well.

In all the hustle and bustle, I managed to meet my future ex-husband. We met when he rang my doorbell on a Sunday afternoon. My little house sat on a lot that the apartment building next door wanted to build an expansion on. It would be a fancy, new modern high rise that would hold 40 new units. Bryan Wiggs was their real estate agent and a very charming, fast talking man.

Initially, I turned down both his request to have dinner and his request to sell my house to the development company he represented. Three days later, he showed up again but this time he brought over dinner. He came prepared with a pre-made basket of fried chicken, mashed potatoes, gravy, corn, biscuits and sweet, tasty coleslaw. The smell of fried chicken and biscuits proved to be irresistible to me so I agreed to eat with him on my patio. It was a warm July evening, so I freshened up my makeup, put on more lipstick, and checked my hair. As he waited, I grabbed two plates, silverware and a cold cola for each of us.

As it turned out, Bryan Wiggs had also brought a handsome offer for my home. Originally, Mother had rented the home for me the ten years later I'd bought it from my landlord and now the lot it sat on was in high demand. While he talked, I handed him a plate, napkin, and a polished fork and knife. He smiled warmly and thanked me profusely. He accepted the cola, pulled off the tab and guzzled it down with barely a breath in-between. After that, he never stopped talking. Perhaps in hindsight, that should have been a red flag. Love is blind, lust is even worse – blind, deaf and incoherent.

Between the dinner and the money he'd presented to me as an offer, my defenses broke down and I felt myself focusing intensely on the curves of his face. He had an extremely toothy and automatic smile, his whole face lit up with perfectly white teeth. He shaved his head nearly bald and had just the barest hint of black curly hair. He stood at least 6' 5" and became my image of my knight in shining armor. As we ate, we caught up on what he didn't already seem to know about me. He knew I had a store and was a successful local businesswoman – an oddity in my time. I told him about my family, just the normal highlights of course. About him, I learned he loved to travel. He'd gotten out of the navy after six years and attended Real Estate school. He enjoyed talking to others and being able to run his own business. Right now his agency was small but he planned on managing a few realtors to form a partnership. He seemed to have worked out what seemed like a solid plan.

When he'd left the next morning, I was 60% ready to sell my little home. The money figures in hand, I spent most of the next week perusing the homes in the country club that were for sale. When Liz and Lois called that week I was still on cloud nine. I had a new boyfriend, and my dream of owning a home in the Greeley Country Club so close I could taste it.

The girls advised me to be cautious, to slow down and of course I promised I would. Their lives were also cruising along. They'd made a recent trip to Reno, Nevada and managed to win $10,000.00 after taxes. They were hoping to buy a new sports car with it. They really wanted to use it to drive down to Los Angeles on weekends and check out the social scene. They'd finally be able to meet some movie stars. Both were dating, but nothing serious – just having fun. The big news, Lois was quitting her job at the City of Monterey and becoming an airline stewardess for Continental Airlines. "What?" I asked. "You quit your job to be an airline stewardess?" "Yes," Lois answered. "I'd like to spend some time in different places, I want to travel," she said. "What does Liz think about that?" I asked. "Put her on the phone please." In the few moments that passed as she transferred the phone to Liz, my mind was still reeling. They'd never spent any time apart. Apart from Liz's often serious but tragic love life, they'd always done things together. "Hello Bea." Liz said. "Will you be okay alone, when she's off to other places?" I asked. "I'm a big girl Bea.

I'll be fine by myself," Liz said. "I'm 30 years old," she said. "She just wants to meet airline pilots," Liz added. At that we both just laughed and I took it as my cue to leave it alone as one of Lois's man meeting schemes.

We finished our conversation and said goodbye. "Tell her good luck and keep me posted," I said. "Sure, "Liz said quietly as she hung up. After I hung up, I started to wonder. Liz seemed short, or even a bit superficial in her conversation with me. There was certainly something up with the two of them, but I tossed out the feeling – or my intuition and got back to planning my dream home. In the long six months it took to finalize the deal on my house, I'd spent every moment of my free time meeting Bryan at houses to look over. Bryan had managed to get a bidding war going between development companies on my house and although it took longer, he actually ended up getting me 20% more than it was worth.

The Greeley Country Club was not the only place to live, but it was an established area near the center of town. It had a golf course, a recreation centers, and a lot of parks and paths. The lots were large and typically included at least an acre of yard that housed an abundance of Blue Spruce trees spaced between colorful blooming trees like crabapple and cherry. The houses I had decorated in this area had all been large, 5-6 bedrooms, dining room, den, and finished basements. I'd fallen in love with nearly every one of them.

However, unfortunately for me homes in the Greeley Country Club rarely went up for sale. As Bryan and I looked and waited, I ended up having to sign a 6 month lease and move into an apartment close to the store. Bryan lived in the same development, just around the other side. We'd meet about five evenings a week, walk around the neighborhood and through the local park, watching the kids play whatever sport happened to be in season and talk. We developed into a couple and since we were together so often, the talk on the street was we were a couple.

Oddly enough, business picked up for both of us. However annoying it was to me personally, that people tended to "favor" women who had what was considered a "normal, proper" relationship are more business worthy, practicality won out and I took all the jobs I could handle. Bryan was also getting the positive fallout, and we'd had to cancel at least two evenings a week just to stay caught up.

Bryan had decided to propose to me after the first month. Although he hadn't found me a house yet, he'd managed to sell several others. He had money in the bank, paid most of his debts, and figured it was the right time but first he had to tell me some news. He'd been married before and had a teenage daughter. It took him a few weeks to get the courage to tell me, and being the talker he was he wiggled it right into a normal dinner conversation without missing a beat. My brain caught up with the conversation when he said his daughter lived in the suburbs outside of Dallas. "Excuse me," I said. "You have a daughter in Dallas?" "How long were you married, why are you divorced, why didn't you tell me this earlier?" I asked. Not that I really cared, I just liked to see him talk his way out of it.

He explained that he met up with his daughter every 3 months for a short trip to the beach, or a drive into Mexico to hang out at a resort. They'd discussed me. Angie was her name and although he knew she was angry at first with his having a girlfriend, she'd grown more receptive to hearing about me. Bryan was sure he talked more than any man he knew, and a few friends had suggested to him that he talked more than a group of women. But, he couldn't seem to stop himself. He wanted to know as much as he could about people. Since his days in the military, talking about even surprisingly simple and mundane subjects helped lessen the fear. He enjoyed trying to bring out the shyer soldiers and getting them to open up. Bryan, you had to say was a true people person. He enjoyed people, loved to learn all he could to piece together life stories. He had dozens of good friends and a few enemies, or those who hated his talking. For Bryan though, there was never any person, at any age, that he couldn't talk to.

He went on to explain that he divorced his wife because she was unfaithful multiple times. I almost spilled my drink.

Some of them were minors he added, with a sour, disgusted look on his face. "I couldn't prove it though, so she got full custody of Angie based on lies about my infidelity," he said. "However, it was Angie's choice," he added painfully. "Angie wanted to be a Dallas Cowboy Cheerleader and since she didn't believe either one of them, she went with her mom to be closer to Dallas," he said quietly. We speak on the phone every week. "What does she think about me?" I asked warily. "She wants to meet you next time," he said smiling. In reality, Angie had agreed to meet me just to shut him up. Bryan was a good father, sending his child support on time without fail and sending money for any extras Angie could come up with. Angie was concerned a new wife would screw that up. But, she managed to avoid meeting me during the 10 years we were married, which was fine by me. Sad, but fine.

Apparently, I learned much later that he'd run his marriage proposal plan past her first. He'd wanted it to be memorable and special. So he planned a July 4th picnic with all our friends. He was baking dessert and had decided mine would be an individually sized coconut cream cake with white and peach frosting. He'd place the ring in the center surrounded by tiny peach carnations and white baby's breath.

The location was a house in the Greeley Country Club he'd put on contract believing it was everything I'd wanted.

He'd even talked the owner into cleaning the entire place and painting the walls beige. He wanted it to be like a brand new canvas to an artist. How could I not love this man? He'd secretly arranged flowers to be delivered along with a new grill as a housewarming gift. He'd make his usual steak and baked potatoes and our few dozen friends were all bringing side dishes. They were all in on the secret and admittedly they did a fine job of keeping it, I had no idea, ever.

The house came up for sale because of a divorce, and was priced at rock bottom. It needed some basic work but was otherwise sound and solid. It had at least four 30' blue spruce trees and a ½ dozen flowering cherry trees, large lawn both front and back and a huge basement. It had all the rooms I had wanted. It looked small from the road, but was built down the side of a hill and was larger than it appeared. He'd put a contract on to hold it for 30 days. He was so excited, he was nearly speechless and it took all he had to hold it in when we were together. Although, I could feel he was somewhat distracted, I assumed it was something else that was consuming his thoughts.

For Bryan, our relationship was perfect. He loved to talk, make friends, host parties and completely enjoyed company. I was quieter, but also loved making new friends and having parties and events to attend. It was a social aspect that I'd never really experienced, and to be honest I rather enjoyed it. I had a small group of friends who were business contacts mostly, or at least started out that way. We created what they call today a social network, minus the computers and cell phones. I was truly on cloud nine socially. However, I was getting restless on the home front. I'd been in that little condo for a year now with no known end in sight. At first I'd resisted re-decorating the bland interior, but my resolve only lasted three months. Bryan and I spent one weekend repainting each room a different shade of red or orange. Marvin came over and hung the blinds in exchange for one of Bryan's grilled steaks and a few beers.

I adored Bryan but he seemed to be getting more closed off. Our intimate moments were still incredible but he'd even backed off of those as well. He usually stayed with me 90% of the time, but now he'd started coming over only twice a week. He seemed fine, and said he was perfectly happy. He was still working on finding my house, we'd even checked out a couple during the week. When I'd driven by that area on Friday I'd taken down the number of a smallish looking red brick with white trim. It looked a bit plain, but the yard was large and it had several beautiful trees. I thought Bryan looked panicked when I handed him the number of the real estate group to call for more information. I couldn't believe I'd seen it before him. It made me think to myself – was Liz right? Was I going too fast? Maybe he really wasn't looking? Maybe I was last on his list? He evaded the subject during the weekend and just said he'd call first thing Monday morning.

Meanwhile, we planned a large BBQ party for July 4th, only two weeks away. Bryan told me he would rent a space and insisted he and his buddies had it all covered. I had to bring paper plates and napkins. I'd also planned to make some creative centerpieces because I was certain they wouldn't have any. To me, he seemed to have something else on his mind. I automatically assumed he'd met someone else. Maybe, he was still in love with his ex-wife? Maybe one of my friends couldn't stand my happiness and was trying to take him away – my mind went on every negative path it could come up with. Our quiet evenings that week ended after dinner and a brief kiss goodnight. I dove into a new project full bore to take my mind off what I expected was an inevitable breakup coming. I am somewhat ashamed to admit that I even went out and bought a few new clothes - nicer, sexier, clothes than I typically wore. The Friday night before July 4th, I put on a nice new outfit, silky underclothes, spruced up the house and made his favorite meal of mac-n-cheese with bacon and broccoli. We snuggled and watched a movie, and he left early – claiming to have a house showing in the early morning before the BBQ.

After he left I followed him, and sure enough he went back home. I hid out in the park across from his unit for nearly 3 hours and he never left, and no one else arrived either. Despondent, I walked back home. I felt guilty for having followed him, but sadder that I was certain he planned to leave me. When I closed my door behind me, I showered and put the silky lingerie in the basket to be cleaned and put away, and poured myself a glass of red wine. I decided to call the girls and check in, as I hadn't heard from them for a couple weeks and I knew they'd probably still be up and with any luck, at home.

Chapter 9

On the fifth ring Liz picked up the phone. "Hello?" she said. "Liz, it's Bea." I answered. "I was having a rough evening and thought I'd check in on you all. How are you doing?" I said. "Oh, we're fine. I'm up for a promotion at the bank. I should hear in a week or so. I'm hoping to move up to Mortgage Loan Officer," she said. "Toby and I are going to Los Angeles for the weekend. We're going to stay and catch a show, and hang out around the pool," she said. She paused a few seconds to see how I'd react. Once an older sister, one is always an older sister. Although, I wanted to tell her to get a separate room, sleep separately – it was really not my place to say. She was an adult, I reminded myself and I certainly wasn't married to Bryan. So, I didn't say anything except, "that's great. Sounds like a wonderful weekend. Will you get a raise with that promotion?" I asked. "Yes, a good one. How's Bryan?" she asked. After a brief pause I blurted out my side of the story for ten minutes, how well we were doing, but yet I hadn't found a home, was tired of the condo, and Bryan was acting funny, not quite himself and not spending as much time with me, and the list went on – a mix of good, bad, and largely assumed negative events that hadn't actually happened yet.

"Well?" I said, "Do you have anything to say?" I asked. "I was waiting for a break in your conversation," Liz said rather smartly. "So, do you talk to each other? Why don't you just ask him after the party tomorrow?" she said. "Maybe he's just busy, or focusing on his work right now," she said. After rolling her answers around in my head for a few minutes, it did sound feasible. He was looking for my home and still working with several paying clients as well. We agreed I should try not to take everything so seriously and stop following him home. I decided it was safer to just change the subject and focus to someone else. "How's Lois doing?" I asked. "She's fine. I heard from her yesterday. She was supposed to be home for the weekend but decided to take an extra shift on a flight to New York and is staying there for 2-3 days," she said. "She seems to be doing fine," she added as if I'd asked a question. We finished with our usual comparison of the weather, price of groceries and a few tidbits about work. Liz would never admit it, but I think she was lonely without Lois, even though she had Toby.

Liz had fully recovered from the car accident. Everything had worked out for her as expected and she didn't appear to have any issues. She'd been out of work for nearly five weeks and the bank happily took her back. Other than Lois's drastic job change, everything had returned to normal. Throughout Liz's recovery Lois had jumped in and taken care of the grocery shopping, and keeping both their hairdos frosted, primped, and sprayed every day. The natural look was not their style. Toby, fortunately had not gotten hurt at all beyond a broken collarbone. He stopped by every couple of days to check on Liz. He'd come with something he'd picked up, usually a hamburger and fries, and sometimes a vanilla shake. He never could find anything except fruit and vegetables to eat at their place, and therefore always brought something for himself and Liz. Of course, unbeknownst to him, Liz would eat a tiny bit of what he'd brought and then throw the bulk of it away after he'd left. Liz was not one to hurt a man's feelings.

Meanwhile, during that time Lois decided she needed to pursue her own dreams rather than, she felt, cleaning up after Liz all the time. Liz this, Liz that – what about Lois? All Liz talked about was what Toby ordered for dinner, what Toby liked to eat, what Toby liked to do, blah, blah, blah, blah. The plain and simple truth was Lois wanted to meet successful, reasonably accomplished, reasonably wealthy men. She wasn't looking for a rich old man, but rather a man close to her age that was at least on his way to becoming wealthy. She wanted to be part of a team that could not be easily derailed by a third party. For example, over the past 10 years she'd worked her way up in the City of Monterey to Senior Accountant and she'd started as an assistant to the Secretary group. She'd only had a high school education and had learned as she went. She'd had a few decent mentors along the way that worked for the city and had seen her as someone with potential. Although she'd had a few tiffs with other coworkers over the years she'd ended up fine. However, she found herself growing more and more restless.

She'd hoped that when they'd moved to Monterey, they'd meet dozens of exciting young men like actors, businessmen, professional ball players – anything but the ordinary "let's get married and have babies" crowd back home. She didn't want to raise anything plant, animal, or human. Truth be told she'd wished she'd gone to college. Alone. In her dreams, she'd pictured herself in the white lab coat and goggles of a scientist. She dreamed of growing cultures, discovering new things, and curing all sorts of disease. Those dreams simply didn't come to pass. In her family, she'd been fortunate just to graduate from high school rather than getting pulled into working the family farm at 15. In our day, succeeding with the family farm was far and away more important than education. She understood that with all of them, it made sense – they had a lot to support. Still, a large part of her resented the pressure to quit school, marry, and raise more kids to work on the farm. None of the boys except Peter ever made it to high school dropping out at age somewhere between 12 and 15. Only Peter, Bea, Liz and Lois graduated with a high school diploma. None of them had even dreamed of college except Lois and Peter.

Peter simply ran out of time once he married and started having his own family. Lois just ran out of energy. Lois originally planned to find a college once she got settled in California. She figured she'd work to make a living and take classes around work hours. The problem was in that day, college courses only happened during the day and Lois was working. She didn't have the luxury of night school or the ability to alter her work schedule around classes. She was also often frustrated that the money she made didn't go nearly as far as she'd expected. Lois was the one who developed a certain level of bitterness towards how things were. She was older than Liz by a mere 9 months and 14 days, but considered herself responsible for Liz's wellbeing and success. She'd managed to get her to move to California with a future plan of sunshine, beaches, parties, and men who didn't farm. Lois had it all planned out, but time after time Liz would fall for another man that wanted her to marry and have children. It amounted to blowing all of Lois's plans as if they didn't matter, as if they weren't as important. It angered Lois more than any of us actually realized. That anger festered into a sense of bitterness that oozed out of every pore of her skin in her later years.

None of us ever recalled Mother complaining about her tasks or life, she simply did what she needed to do. However, we all noticed on occasion she'd be starting off into space thinking of something that had nothing to do with slopping pigs, hanging laundry and the rest of her endless chores. She'd be lost in thought, automatically hanging clothes on the line like a robot and staring towards the mountains, a few tears trickling down her face. We never did know what she dreamed about and she'd never say. She'd just smile, rub our heads and send us off to do another chore.

It seemed to Lois that Liz spent most of her time and energy falling head over heels in love with one boy or another. Liz fell for anyone who spoke kindly to her or looked her way. As a child, Lois would stomp off in a huff whenever Liz and her latest beau would be hanging out on the swing, or chatting during recess at school.

Lois focused on working and her dreams of independence. She'd be free of the farm, the dirt, the chores and all the never-ending reminders that her purpose was to find a husband and raise kids. No one ever asked her if that's what she wanted, they all assumed. It bothered all of us girls, but not to the same extent. Lois never dated in high school and refused to be setup. When Mother passed away and Gracie came rapidly thereafter, her connection to home was broken. Once Mother was gone, we all realized how much she'd done, not only the physical chores, but all the other thingsto hold the family together and help them find their way along. She was the only one that made Lois feel loved.

When Gracie started critiquing their clothes, their hair, the way they walked, not to mention how they did laundry and peeled potatoes, that'd been the last straw for Lois. She easily convinced Liz to pack their few things and move in with me in town. The plan was to work and save their money for two tickets to California. They'd told only Peter because honestly he's the only one who really noticed their existence. He'd practically raised all of us in-between farming. Lois was certain Father had not ever noticed their absence. He'd never spoken to them before, so it wasn't high on their list of concerns that he wouldn't speak to them later.

The three of us consoled ourselves against his disinterest by finishing school and finding careers so we could support ourselves and never set foot on that farm again. To be fair, Father was a decent man who occasionally drank too much, and yelled a lot. We did always have food on the table, decent clothes and shoes which made us very lucky in reality. A lot of kids survived with a great deal less. Although he yelled a lot, he never got violent with the girls only with his sons. Blessings are blessings after all, and we were blessed in our general security.

After Lois spent a school session studying the western United States in geography, she made a plan to move to California as soon as she turned 16. She'd spent days copying the map from her schoolbook to paper that she stuck together to form a full California map that hung on her wall. She dreamed of the beaches and being near the ocean. Her dreams included palm trees, warm weather, sunbathing days with a picnic lunch and something to read. She circled the cities of San Diego, Monterey, Carmel, and Los Angeles – one of those would be her future home. California represented a place far away from the farm fields of northern Colorado. All the movie stars, radio stars – all the famous people she knew of lived there. She and Liz saved the majority of their Christmas money, and any other extra money they'd earn for their one-way train tickets to freedom.

They had it well planned until Liz got caught up with Robert Gaines, "Robbie" as most people called him. He was a popular young man who excelled in basketball, baseball, and football. Robbie stood about 6' 5" with dark brown eyes, and brown hair – he was by far the handsomest young man in high school. He stood at least 6 inches taller than Liz with her auburn hair and green eyes. Lois watched Liz follow him around during school, after school, and at each athletic event Liz could get to. Father let her out of chores while Mother stayed up late sewing her a few new dresses for any occasion she may need one. Mother even bought several from the Sears catalog! Unheard of in our day, the majority of our clothes were made by hand by Mother and our two older sisters – store bought clothes were a luxury. Admittedly we all benefited from it as Mother made sure we all got at least something to make it fair.

One morning after hearing about wedding plans, wedding food, wedding dresses, Lois and Liz had a loud fight. Peter was sent in to break it up. It was a Saturday morning and I caught a ride from town out to the farm to visit Mother and enjoy the family meals I missed living in town. Peter had gone to town and dropped Liz off with Roger as an escort to watch the baseball game Robbie was playing in. I'd caught a ride back with him. I could tell by Liz's irritated look and extra quiet demeanor that'd she and Lois had gotten into a disagreement. "Did you two have a fight?" I'd asked Liz. "No, she's just jealous of mine and Robbie's love is all. She wants me to just give it all up for her silly dream of living in California without a man. She's impossible." Liz said in a rant as she and Roger exited the truck and Peter and I headed back to the farm. Once we arrived, I headed down to the creek, Lois's favorite spot on the farm when we were growing up.

When I saw her, her eyes were bloodshot from crying and she was at the burn can fanning the flames of Liz's portion of the California plan. "Are you okay kiddo," I asked. "She's such a fool. Robbie doesn't care about her but all she does to run around after him just like we agreed we would never do," Lois said. "She doesn't even care about her promise or pact, we had an agreement after all – a sworn pact," she added. "All she talks about is Robbie, what Robbie wants her to do, how he likes her hair, what he wants her to bake for him, and then the wedding plans. He hasn't even asked her to marry him but she goes on like it's the best thing ever. She's stupid." Personally, I didn't think it was stupid, but Liz saw an opportunity she thought was better. She was in love with Robbie, or at least that's what we assumed. We were all too young to really know what that meant exactly except for marriage. For Liz it was a way to get out of the house, and maybe she really did love Robbie or believed she did. It was hard to say, all she wanted to talk about was wedding dresses and hairstyles when I saw her as well. But, she was young and in love at least as far as any of us knew. Most of us didn't believe the girls would ever move to California – it was a childish dream. I was as guilty as the rest of the family believing it was only a childish dream. The girls would grow up and marry a local man and raise children. I believed the same for myself, but for me I'd meet my husband at work.

For Lois however, California was no childish dream. Her savings, her plan and her pacts were serious. She swore to me and anyone else who would listen that she'd be there by the time she was 16. Ultimately she was a few years off but not by much. As we finished up the chickens, goats, and pigs and the afternoon faded away I headed back to help with dinner. Lois said she'd be in after a few minutes. I believed her and headed in. It'd been awhile since I'd visited Mother and I'd certainly missed Mother's dinners. I'd been helping finish off the bread and busied myself setting the table and gathering the drinking glasses and silverware. Over the years, Mother had developed a voice her children and husband could hear several acres away. She called inside and outside for Lois, no Lois came. It was Lois's job to make the vegetables. I set off upstairs to check for her. In her room the

California map remained intact on the wall but Liz's name was scrubbed off.

The room also had a string, the cotton string the boys used when working with the cattle, carefully hooked with tacks and dividing the room down the middle. Each girl's belongings were on either side of the line. It appeared that they'd had a typical teenage fight inevitable, I believed as we each made our way through adolescence to our separate adult lives. As teenagers I guess some of us move on through our life experiences and others believe certain events cannot be overcome. It was five hours before Peter and Lois came through the door, and well after dinner.

They were both covered in engine grease and oil. The story they gave Mother was Liz had been angry with Lois because she refused to be part of the wedding Liz was planning. Lois had needed to get away and so had gone down to work on some equipment repairs. It sounded plausible and Mother put together their dinner without a word. Peter however wouldn't look me in the eye. I knew the story was only half true and my intuition bristled – the hairs on the back of my neck stood on end. What the heck had they really gotten into? Peter never diverged from his story – even though we both knew it wasn't totally true. He maintained his stance when he drove me back to town Sunday morning while the rest of the family attended church. "Don't worry about it, " he said. "She was upset, was getting into trouble – but we got it fixed. No harm, no foul," he said. It was a phrase he always used when he was fixing errors made by his younger siblings. Despite Peters reassurances, my feelings of, not evil necessarily, but something bad persisted.

I gave Peter a hug and a kiss as he dropped me off at my little house in town and turned back to return home. I got into my Sunday chores and worked until those bad gut feelings were gone. I didn't even remember it until recently when Liz and Toby had the car accident.

Chapter 10

After Robbie's death Liz did her chores like a machine. She took down Lois's string dividing their room in half and added herself back to the California map. The family in general coped by not mentioning him at all. To me, and I imagined Liz as well, it was like living in a fish bowl. Her own world flowed around her as if nothing significant had happened. No waves, no ripples, nothing. Instead of making it better, I think it made it worse. For Liz, it felt like the world never stopped, not a pause, not a burp or moment of silence – everything went on. Peter had taken her to the service and I had met them both there. Afterwards as the family cleared, Liz stared down at the casket as the warm, dry summer breeze blew through the loose hair on her face and dried her silent tears. After twenty minutes, she abruptly threw in an arrangement of flowers she'd been holding and headed for the car. Peter and I rose from the bench we'd found nearby in the shade and followed her. There was no sound except our footfalls on the moist, wet grass. I'm sure she didn't hear my goodbyes or my weak words of encouragement and hope. When a loved one dies, there's a span of time where there really is simply nothing to say or be said. I waved softly to Peter as he drove off.

After a few weeks, Liz and Lois were back on their California planning. Liz took a job as a bank teller in town and finished school on the side with the help of a few understanding teachers. Lois found herself a job just a few weeks later as a secretary at the city water department just 3 blocks from the bank and 4 blocks from my shop. We were all townies at last! Three times a week we each walked the two blocks to the city park and ate our lunch on one of the benches. It may have still smelled like a farm in town, but it was still town and we were finally officially city girls! They saved nearly all their money for California almost religiously. They'd take turns embellishing ocean stories and what they'd do when they swam in the sea like mermaids. They built it up and up until it was nearly a fairy tale – and I did the same with my dreams of living in the country club. The country club homes were spacious and were surrounded by acres of green grass and large shade trees. There were parks, and sidewalks and separate shops, a golf course, restaurants and a swimming pool. None of which I'd ever actually seen but could only imagine.

I'm still not sure why we ever wanted to be so far away from our farming roots. It was good for us, and to us, for the most part. For myself, I so hated the smell of sweat, blood, manure and bugs. All I wanted to be was clean, cool, and smell like perfume. I loved living in town and working. Here I was still close enough to family, and yet still distant enough to feel independent.

When our mother died, all of our worlds collided and then collapsed when Gracie came. We all changed, dissipated, and moved on. Maybe it was Gracie, but maybe it was just timing. No matter what happens the sun still rises in the morning and sets in the evening without pause. No time to reassemble the pieces before another day starts and ends. Life runs over you and goes on. You pick yourself back up, dust yourself off and get moving again. Thank goodness for Peter, because without mother I was lost in a deep, dark hole. He was always my hand up as long as he was around. He'd help you up, dust you off, and set you back in motion almost as if he was setting irrigation pipes. Enough serious reflection on history, let's get back to my big day!

It was July 3rd and I had one day left before our summer party. I had boxes of centerpieces, napkins folded like flower petals all in peach and white. There were streamers, balloons, and plates – all the peach and white I could find. I'd had to settle for clear glasses, but other than that it was perfect. I'd even managed to order tablecloths to sell at the store. I'd re-done the front display window in a peaches and milk theme – the perfect bridge between farm and the sweet smell of clean. I remained suspicious of Bryan, but put the thoughts and doubts aside as I worked on the decorations. I enjoyed the work and the mental diversion. We planned on him picking me up that morning so we'd only take up a single parking space. I assured him over the phone that night that there were only four boxes. I slept in until noon on the

4th and then spent nearly an hour on my hair alone. When Bryan showed up promptly at 1pm he was nervous and bursting with energy. He stacked two boxes on top of each other and nearly them out to his car. I wasn't really sure if he was just nervous, hyper, or restless. He drove and talked non-stop the entire way, which honestly was at least 20 minutes. As we stopped in front two cars were already there. It was his two grilling buddies Mark and Chris setting up the grill.

The house itself looked brighter, the red brick had been cleaned and the trim freshly painted. The lawn was trimmed and green. Mark and Chris had setup 5 tables with metal folding chairs. There were coolers filled with ice, pop, and beer and separate jugs of lemonade and ice tea. Bryan plopped my boxes next to me and headed for the grill, grabbing one beer as he passed by the first cooler. The three of them started talking and gesturing like soldiers discussing battle plans.

I proceeded to decorate each table with a tablecloth, cluster of napkins, and a centerpiece. It looked absolutely perfect! I made my way to the powder room and arrived to greet the guests with fresh perfume and lipstick. Groups of people chatted and churned around the shady backyard. One could easily move from sun to shade as they pleased. A few children played ball down in the corner where the lawn dropped gradually over a small hill. They took turns chasing and kicking the ball from one end of the fence to the other. A couple of women eyed their children as they mingled and chatted. As the sun began to set, Bryan turned on the porch lights and the remaining guests gradually moved in under the light. I was starting to get tired and finally sat down near Bryan and the grilling crew. A few hours of beer and pop had them floating between wired and mellow.

Bryan moved closer and gave me a hug and kiss – quite a kiss for a crowd and it left me slightly embarrassed. As I looked down, I caught the image of Mark and Chris coming behind me with a huge cake ablaze with candles. It wasn't my birthday, but right for me they headed and stopped. Bryan got down on one knee and my heart jumped. He blew out the candles and handed me a tiny round box. I opened it slowly and inside a huge diamond ring sat and stared back at me. Huge and round, it sparkled in its gold setting. As I sat there staring at it, Bryan picked it up with his long, tanned fingers and said, "Well, will you marry me?" I stared at him for an eternity, people waited on my answer so quietly I could hear the birds twittering as they flew past. My mind raced through images of my family, my harsh but good father, my hard working mother, Peter, my sisters and troubled brothers. I had my doubts, but all that came out was "Yes." At the moment, the lights in the house all went on and illuminated a silver bow running from one end to the other. "It's all yours," Bryan said. "The house – I bought it for you, well – you bought it actually. Surprise! What do you think?"

I didn't hear or see anyone after that. I got up slowly, rolled the diamond ring around on my finger and Bryan and I walked through the entire house. Granted I'd seen it once before several weeks earlier, and it was in the country club. If I'd built a house, that wouldn't have been it. It had a lot of small rooms, but that could be changed. It was deceptively large. The front appeared smaller, but the back rolled down the side of a hill finishing off in a finished walk out basement with its own deck and patio. As I walked and stared, Bryan went on how he'd had it painted beige so I could start fresh. If I didn't like the hardwood floors he'd get carpet in, whatever I wanted. I found the last corner bedroom in the basement, hugged him and gave him a kiss he'd never forget. We made love right there, quickly, passionately, beautifully and perfectly. The party was closing up as we walked back onto the back patio. We said our goodbyes and well wishes and walked to the house, locked the doors and headed upstairs where Bryan had the master bedroom already prepared.

It was a memorable holiday weekend and we never left the house. By Monday it was back to work and then the packing and moving started. My coworkers had been at the party so they already knew about my news but they graciously cooed and awed over my ring and the event again anyway. As I settled down to work, my first call was to Peter and my second to Lois and Liz. Of course, they were all at work – so I called them back that evening. It was a good week at the shop. We got several large orders and sales from my peach and white collection.

In the evenings, I poured over catalogs and books putting together the plan for my new home. I could get most of the supplies wholesale from the shop. In two weeks I had a plan and was unloading boxes as the painters finished up and made way for the carpet installers. It would have been a crime to cover up the mahogany hardwood floors, so I had them refinished. The new carpet replaced the old in the upstairs bedrooms and basement. I spent more weekend time sorting through antique markets, magazines and thrift shops looking for unique items. One for the store and one for me was how it generally went.

Bryan and I moved in the same weekend as the carpet installers finished up. He set up his office and worked half the time from home. He cleared out when I was decorating and worked on the lawn. We met neighbors and fussed over the house, made love at least once in every room, and the next thing we knew summer was over and it was nearly Halloween. We finally set our date for December 28th and I started planning my wedding. Evelyn, Peter's wife was so excited she ended up doing 90% of the work. She'd put together nice events for all our siblings at some time or the other, and couldn't wait to help me with my wedding. I picked out a simple dress and she picked out everything else. It worked out rather well because with the shop I didn't have much time to invest in it. We traded out services in the end, I got her some good deals on items she wanted, and she did my wedding. We only butted heads on the location.

Evelyn went right for our hometown Lutheran church and I wanted the country club. We ended up at the country club married by the Lutheran pastor. Since neither of us was Lutheran, he performed the service as a favor to Evelyn. Although I believed in God, I wasn't a fan of the Lutheran church. Their rules I found overbearing, rusty and old – serve the man, serve the father, then the husband is what they tried to beat into your brain. My version was serve your self. In my mind, that service to men is what killed my mother or at minimum, what caused her to work from dusk to dawn taking care of her husband and sons. For her it'd been normal, but for me it appeared simply unfair.

For Peter & Evelyn's sake I swallowed my resentment and went with the pastor. As the pastor spoke the words to "honor and obey" Bryan winked at me and I rolled my eyes. We had the reception at our home and then took off to spend the weekend in Estes Park. We had rented a quiet little cabin in the heart of Rocky Mountain National Park.

After life settled down again and we both got back to working, we agreed to meet for dinner every night by 7pm.

Bryan did the cooking and I did the cleanup. It was a good deal. After I got caught up again at the shop, I called Peter and checked in. Evelyn was rested up and ready to go again as she reminded me to tell Lois and Liz she was available. I promised I would. In fact, the last time I'd spoken to the girls was to give them my good news and tell them to check their mail for the wedding invitation and photos from the party. Neither of them had attended the wedding, but had sent a card and gift together. Liz answered finally the second time I'd dialed. "Hello, how are you doing, did you get my pictures from the party, what did you think?" I blurted out before she'd even had time to acknowledge me. I paused. "Liz, are you there?" I said.

"Yes, Bea – I was just waiting for you to burn down a bit," she said. Gosh, I wish I had your energy. The ring looks beautiful and the party looked absolutely ornate, so sorry we missed it. I'm glad the wedding went well and we'll be looking for those pictures. "What's up with you two these days, catch me up," I said.

Liz was busy at the bank. She'd gotten the promotion and had become the first female mortgage loan officer. She was doing quite well. She'd gotten a couple bonuses and a raise already. She had now set her sights on becoming the next branch director in a few years. She'd had a bit of a health problem, but nothing to be concerned about, she lied trying to convince me. "Did you go to a doctor," I asked?

You and Lois are just the same, doctor this, doctor that. I finally got tired of Lois's nagging and went. Turns out she had a tumor in her left leg and had it removed right during my wedding. It had been malignant and about the size of a baseball. She was tired, but felt better after it was out. "Sorry I couldn't attend your wedding," she added. "Oh my God, why didn't you tell me," I practically screamed at the phone as a slow, creeping anger started to build. "I could have helped, postponed the wedding," I added. "No, no it's all fine now. Lois stayed home that week and carted me back and forth. Lois even did all the cooking and cleaning, believe it or not," Liz added. I felt both insulted and hurt. Liz had never mentioned any illness at all. It was as if they were pulling away, even from me.

I stifled my hurt and played positive giving her all the details I could in the space of fifteen minutes. I discovered Toby had broken up with her when he'd found out she had cancer. He didn't even wait to see how bad it was, he left at the very idea of it. Liz responded with all the emotion of a person who'd just scraped a pimple off their face – not broken up with a serious boyfriend. Lois had gotten angry and she'd taken a scissor to all Toby's clothes and thrown them out in the lawn. As he picked up what he could, she soaked him with the garden hose. It had been quite a scene, and I could clearly picture it in my mind. "So, he was living with you all?" I asked. "Yes, it's the 70s, Bea, not the 50s. Besides it's better to know them before you marry them," she added. "Good talking to you, here's Lois," she said. I heard what sounded like a raccoon wrestling with a cord and some muffled voices and then finally, "Hi Bea. Congratulations on the wedding," Lois said in her best snide voice. "We're so looking forward to seeing the photos. We'd have been there except for Liz's little operation," she added slurring her words. She sounded drunk. I paused and tried to figure out why they hadn't told me about Liz's tumor and why they seemed so distant and aloof?

Lois continued talking on like a woman to a small child, cooing and giggling and telling me stories as if I were 10 years old in a time where cancer and weddings were not pivotal events in life. If we had still been 10 years old, I'd have grabbed her by the shoulders and we'd had a yelling, screaming, and hair pulling fight. We'd have worked it out right then and there and probably come out as closer friends. As it was, it seemed we'd grown apart or crossed a boundary. I'd supported their choices and defended their dreams and now I only got empty conversation that was completely superficial and devoid of any real feeling. I always called, they never called me unless it was an emergency. I found myself seething with anger, and it was building up with each little giggle that grated on my nerves. I quietly hung up the phone.

I cried for exactly 20 minutes. I cried loudly until I could only breathe in gasps. Then it was over, I felt like a weight had been lifted from my shoulders, a burden I'd dragged along for decades was finally gone. I'd worried over those two my entire life. I was always mending their fences, listening to their dreams and their lives and encouraging them to do whatever they wanted. Had they ever worried about me? Yes, I remembered our childhood pact not to marry. I fondly remembered getting done with chores and heading out to the creek to play. However, mostly I watched over them making sure they didn't get hurt, didn't get in over their heads. I'd even let them live with me when they were between home and California. I'd covered their rent, and their needs. They'd said "thank you" at the time but now I was not sure they'd ever meant it. They never went out of their way for me. I'd been right there for Liz's recovery with each car accident, I'd been there every time to defend Lois from allegations of wrong doing at every turn. I was a bridge for them, a way to cross over without getting wet. A way to the other side that was safe and reliable. Had they ever even noticed?

Maybe in reality they did. A normal person like myself just couldn't tell. Besides, at this point, I was on such a rant all of life seemed stacked against me. The one most important moment of my life and they'd ignored it. I went on with myself for several hours this way until finally I picked myself up, showered, and made my favorite meal of kraut burgers and pumpkin pie. My home glowed with warmth and color and smelled the part too. I chased away the chemical smell of new carpet and paint and replaced it with two simple and honest smells- pumpkin pie and bread. Maybe that's the joy my mother had that none of us noticed or understood. At the end of every day she cooked and we all ate. The smells from her kitchen were delicious and intoxicating – totally taken for granted. She baked doughnuts on Sunday mornings along with blinna and fruit. It was incredible. She'd had 10 children and she'd helped me get my dream of a house in town despite the family's disapproval. At that moment, I realized again how much I missed her and how I truly knew so little about her. She'd loved us all. And as Bryan walked through the door that evening, I realized how much he'd done for me. We were together, our own family complete in our peaches and white dream home. They didn't call me back and I didn't call them either.

Chapter 11

Meanwhile, back on the coast Lois rattled on for fifteen or twenty minutes to herself. She'd pause long enough to drink another swig of wine and start up again. This had been her first year as a flight attendant. She loved it. She had dated more handsome men than she'd ever imagined possible. Some were older, younger, but most hovered around her age. All, she bragged were pilots. The silence of the phone finally jogged her from her reverie. "That bitch hung up on me," she screamed across the apartment. "Well, no wonder you're drunk. Go to bed and sleep it off," Liz said. Lois slammed down the phone and wobbled on her 6-inch heels down the short hall to her room and slammed the door. Liz continued to roll her hair when she wasn't rolling her eyes. Since Lois had been jetting here and there as a flight attendant, Liz spent many evenings taking phone messages from men all over the country.

Liz had always been the pretty one, the one everyone fussed over and the one who always had the solid, popular, going places boyfriend. She would have been married first except for Robbie's death and she could have married Toby. Why did it matter anyway? She was a working woman who loved her career and loved the bank she worked for. It was important, exciting and above all she made her own money and ran her own life. Within relationships, something always held Liz back from making that final commitment. Fate, pain, accidents, maybe even guilt? "Guilt over what?" she asked herself. Perhaps it was guilt over leaving Lois behind to fend for herself? Lois could fend for herself just fine. Maybe it was guilt over a childhood pact not to marry? No, that'd just been a game Lois had always taken way too seriously. Maybe it was fear of getting her hopes up and then something happening to put her back at square one? Life is often like a game of Parcheesi - you almost get home and then have to start over again. It's exhausting.

Neither of them was getting any younger and she'd lost her patience with men. They should have gone to Bea's wedding after all, she sighed. She could have had the cancer surgery later, but since it was malignant she didn't want to chance it. She just didn't want to go back to Greeley, not now, not later, not ever.

She pulled her hair a bit harder as she rolled it and pinned shorter clips of hair around her face just to the point where it caused a little pain. Not one single hair would be straight in the morning. She scrubbed her face with her own mixture of avocados and cucumbers and polished it off with a healthy layer of lotion. She brushed her teeth meticulously for 5 minutes and settled into her exercise routine of a variety of stretches. She didn't want muscle, but she wanted to stay as lean as possible. Quite a beauty routine for a woman who was tired of men, she chuckled quietly to herself as she walked down the short hall and turned into her bedroom, quietly closing the door.

They'd both eaten dinner a few minutes before I had phoned, Lois washing hers down with a second bottle of white wine. They'd skipped dessert so there was no need to reduce the number of calories tonight, a welcome break from throwing up at least half what she'd eaten. As far as Liz was concerned it was normal, an effective way to reduce calories.

What was she to do about Lois's drinking? Ever since she'd become a flight attendant, Lois had significantly increased her wine intake. Fortunately, Liz did all the driving, so as long as Lois could wobble from one place to another it would be fine, Liz mused. Likely it was just a passing phase. It concerned her because all the brothers had a propensity to drink and it never ended well. They'd make up stories and excuses to cover just about anything. It had been one of the reasons they'd left home. Liz didn't miss that dark, broody feeling that usually turned from a loud argument into a fist fight or brotherly brawl outside in the dirt. It usually ended with Peter hosing down the participants and sending or dragging each one to bed. As she'd watched Lois on the phone, that familiar, dark and brooding look colored her otherwise bright blue eyes and made her feel depressed. What was she to do with her sister? She couldn't just hose her down.

When Liz poured out the rest of the bottle of wine, Lois decided to cut the evening short and wobbled down to her room and slammed the door. She undressed and climbed into the bed and then curled up her tiny frame and fell asleep. "Thank God for California, you don't even need a blanket," she whispered to herself as she drifted off to sleep. Those were her parting words for the evening and much of the following day.

Liz rose the next morning and went to the store. Overnight, she'd decided she needed a hobby. She needed a hobby that would be useful and keep her entertained on the weekends. She enjoyed spending time at home, so baking seemed the way to go. She took her time as she stopped in town to shop and wound up with three cookbooks for beginners. Liz decided more beach time sounded good too, so she bought a new bathing suit and her first pair of bright red tennis shoes for walking. Then, she happened upon two new outfits and headed to the grocery. At the grocery store, she bought the ingredients for a lasagna dinner.

As she checked out, Liz was thinking about how they'd lived two blocks from the beach for many years now and had only gone there on weekends in the summer. No more, she'd walk after work on her way home and take in the setting sun, the fresh air, and all the sights and sounds of the beach at dusk. Her previous beach excursions consisted of sunbathing and trying to find dates. However, now that'd she'd been through several serious relationships (at least she'd considered them serious), - who knew what Toby or Robbie had thought.

Toby and she dated almost three years, had gotten engaged and then the car accident threw everything off. Toby disappeared when she'd gone in for a cancer/tumor test and she'd never heard from him again. He'd paid the hospital bills for the car accident and her cancer treatment. He'd never picked up the few shirts and toiletries he'd kept at the house. He'd never called, and when she'd made two attempts to call him, no one had answered. Liz and Toby had spent weekends at different coastal bed & breakfast inns and enjoyed many romantic dinners. She sighed remembering all the good memories of those times and then marveled at how quickly he'd left when it seemed she was sick. He didn't even wait around long enough to see how serious it was. Here it had been a year, and so far she was cancer free. Liz celebrated her cancer free first year by tackling two new hobbies - cooking and beach walking. She was quite proud of herself. She was healthy, had two new hobbies and combined with her new promotion to a mortgage loan officer it made her life seem quite rosy.

As she pulled the car into the drive, a cab was just driving out. Lois waved as they passed in the drive. Liz waved back. Well, she'd just pack up the leftovers and eat them for the rest of the week she muttered as she carried the groceries and her new things into the house. As she set the bags on the kitchen table, she saw Lois's note. Lois wrote she'd be back on the following friday. "Think about going up for the weekend to Carmel, my treat," she wrote. Followed by, "have a good week." Liz crumpled up the note and tossed it in the trash. Carmel this coming weekend would be perfect - and it fit into her beach walking plans too. As she unloaded groceries, holding back the ingredients for her lasagna, she hummed along with whatever songs popped into her head, as she rolled, stuffed, baked and sauced. As it baked, she showered and pin curled her hair for Monday. All clean and ready to relax, she took her dinner to the couch and leisurely ate while perusing the remainder of the Sunday newspaper. She finished eating, cleaned her dishes and headed for bed. All in all, she liked her prospects.

Chapter 12

Lois's head pounded when her alarm clock rang mid-morning. She had to cut down on the wine in the evenings she told herself. She'd work on it starting after this next trip. She didn't like being the goody-two-shoes in the group who didn't drink. The groups seemed to form around the pilot and the head stewardess. Over the past year, she'd finally found a group that she felt comfortable and got along with. She now had three groups that she tended to bounce between. Her coworkers at the city had found her "difficult to work with." It wasn't her she'd always claimed, if only her former manager could see her now. She was in three groups and in demand. Sure, she'd had a few run-ins with one or two fellow stewardesses and a couple pilots. However, she'd persevered. She didn't have many personal or ethical rules except one - don't date men in your own group.

She certainly enjoyed gossiping about eligible pilots, and she'd dated several. Most had been pleasant but were lacking the passion she'd hoped for. Mostly, Lois enjoyed having a good time. However, each happy hour usually involved at least one drink with coworkers. Eventually, her drinking soda rule turned into drinking just one glass of wine. Then, she changed it from one glass of wine to no more than 4.

She'd dated 7 men over the past couple years, but only one tempted her heart.

London was his name, and he had distinct possibilities. The honk of the taxi horn woke her from her reverie and she grabbed her purse as she scratched out a quick note to Liz. She'd actually have a long weekend layover coming up and wanted to spend the weekend with Liz at the beach sunbathing and shopping. Liz was so serious about her work though, Lois wasn't sure she'd go for it. Lois wanted a chance to brag and talk about her love life. Lois was enjoying being the one with all the suitors now. She waved as the taxi passed Liz. Lois was off again and this time the team included London. London was her new favorite even if he was only a co-pilot. He was completely dreamy. He worked hard, listened well, and was always polite. He also had excellent taste in wine. She hadn't succeeded in getting him to ask her out as yet, but Lois believed she was close.

Granted he was already married to another stewardess, but rumor had it the marriage was close to being a bust, and Lois was poised and ready to pick up the pieces. Either way, she planned to pursue the opportunity. Now to be fair, Lois was not looking to get married, she wanted experiences, as she called it. We'll let her explain herself from here because I as her older sister, never really understood her motives or what exactly she was looking for.

Let me give you my side - I'm Lois, independent, perhaps slightly bitter after spending most of my youth doing farm chores that basically amounted to caring for everyone and everything besides myself. Chickens, cows, crops, a distant and cold father and several older brothers all expected to be cared for at once and constantly. The boys always got the good chores - driving tractors, fixing equipment, and driving the delivery trucks. As girls, we got stuck endlessly washing clothes, stealing eggs from hostile chickens, and floundering through mud and muck to feed and care for cattle. The only time we got away from the house was for an hour, maybe two in the late afternoon. It was that wonderful time between when the morning chores were done and before the evening chores started. It was these rare times when us girls would hitch a ride on the tractor from Peter and he'd drop us at the creek. We'd eat our packed lunch that we'd quickly thrown together from breakfast scraps and eat while we chased toads, fish and generally enjoyed the shade and each other's company. We talked, relaxed and basically did nothing but what we wanted to.

After the death of our mother, Father in his infinite wisdom, wasted no time bringing home a stepmother we had no interest in. For my own mother, yes I would cook, clean and serve the boys like we were hired hands, but like hell I was going to do that for Gracie. From the day she stepped in the door, Gracie started barking orders. Granted she took over most of the baking, but she ate most of it too. Bea had already escaped home, and Liz and I began to quietly make our plans to move on. Most of our brothers and sisters had already split off their families into their own farms. Even Peter who was Father's anchor bought a place shortly after Gracie's arrival that was just a few miles down the road. The farm was expanding and contracting seemingly at the exact same time. Remarkably Father drew up legal papers dividing the existing farm between the boys, naturally nothing for us girls as we were expected to find a suitable man and marry. Liz and I made an effort to get a few acres that included our favorite part of the creek, even got all the boys to agree. We could live between farms and have our own little acre to be. But, night after night we got the same response. "No, you girls need to marry, women don't need land, you need husbands," they'd say.

Fed up, we moved in with Bea in town. We'd get our own land somewhere more valuable than a farm. My focus turned again to California and it became to me a goal rather than a childhood dream. I wanted to find a place near the beach and spend every day running through the waves, searching for seashells and just lying in the sun. I wanted it more than anything else I could think of, and certainly more than I wanted to marry any of the hayheads around Greeley. The absolute last thing I wanted to be was a farmer's wife. Liz was on the same page with me when her attention wasn't diverted by some idiot boy she claimed to have fallen in love with. She couldn't seem to focus. But I did. I was never going to marry, and for once I'd work for myself first and foremost. The baking and cleaning I did would be for me and not my thankless, unfeeling Father and complacent brothers.

Bea was so lucky that Mother had gotten her that house in town before she'd died. Liz was focused on marrying Robbie and could barely think of anything else. She spent four years running after that dweeb like a starving dog following a slab of bacon. Liz was a fool. I finally gave up on her and just planned California for myself. I had calculated it out. It would take me a year to raise enough funds to take the train to California, find a place to stay and get work. Bea despite her annoying mother-like tendencies gave me a good start. I was able to live rent free that first year. Peter also helped me out, bless his heart. He showed me how to maintain a car. I helped him with the oil and filter changes whenever he needed a smaller pair of hands. I was perfect for the job. It was the only time I really felt I had done anything of value. Once I got a taste of that, it was too late to be someone's farm wife slaving away until I died.

As soon as I'd unpacked at Bea's, the next day I hit the pavement to find a job. I had been good at math in school and finally convinced the city office to hire me as an assistant. Within two months I moved from assistant to executive assistant and then to an accountant. My boss was an independent woman too. We talked about how the working world functioned and she taught me accounting techniques I could not learn in school. We became fast friends and I even bit my tongue and participated as a bridesmaid in her wedding that fall. I was both surprised and excited when she returned to work after a long honeymoon. She was amazing. Emily was her name and she was impressive. Emily was also the friend I needed with Liz so focused on planning her and Robbie's wedding.

It was so annoying. I'd have a wonderful, intelligent day at work and come and have to listen to Liz spend hours trying to decide on which flowers to put in the centerpieces of the reception tables at her wedding. She move on to the towels she wanted to buy for their house, what curtains she'd get, and finally the plants she'd have in the front yard. I think Robbie could have been exchanged for any man, Liz was more in love with the shopping and decorating of the house than she was with Robbie. He knew it too. Robbie flirted with any girl that came into his father's car dealership. I'm certain he slept with several of them as there was usually one who came up missing – as in "visiting their sister in Cleveland." Right. More like having the baby somewhere else so no one in town would know. If Liz had married him, she'd have the house and all the trappings but he'd have his girls on the side too. I could see it. The family all knew it but they didn't care. Robbie's family had money and she'd be married off. As long as she was married off they didn't really care whom it was to. It infuriated me so much that I threw all my energy into working and saving so I could escape. I wasn't about to stand by and watch Liz ruin her life.

Bea wasn't much help either. She was always cooing over fancy materials and linens, spending entire days shopping and staring at jewelry and dresses like a young girl. She may have been working too, but I had no doubt Bea would marry the first man who asked her. Disgusting. Aside from my brother Peter, I kept all other men away from me. Peter was the only male in my life that had ever been supportive or caring. He never gave any indication to me that I couldn't do anything I wanted to. He'd teach me anything I wanted to learn about tractors and equipment without any hesitation. Always encouraged me to try new things and be what I wanted to be. He never treated us like we only existed to marry. For me, Peter was a bright light in a fog of pain and boredom.

Sometimes at night, Peter would tune the radio in to stations for news updates on the war or whatever else was going on. There was a weekly segment about pilots. I learned about Amelia Earhart and decided that I wanted to be a pilot. I had no idea how to get there, but at the time I wanted to be just like Amelia Earhart. On the day Liz and I moved into town with Bea, Peter gave me some brochures he'd picked up in town. One was for the Navy and one was for the Air Force. Each had pilot training and a base in California. Now, it didn't say they had female pilots but the brochure didn't say they didn't either. I believed I could do it and I would. Now California didn't have just the ocean, beaches and sunshine it also had the promise of flight. I wasn't sure how exactly I was going to be a pilot, but my first step was getting there. Granted, in hindsight my initial plan may have been overly ambitious because in the 1950;s women weren't allowed to be pilots in either the Navy or the Air Force. Sad, but true. I bolted from the recruiting center when they'd told me that. Tears streamed from my eyes and I thought my whole world was over. Bea comforted me and set me straight. Work, save your money and learn to fly she'd told me. Eventually, I'd buy me own plane and fly whenever I wanted and wherever I could go.

That dream did not exactly work out. But, I am a stewardess and I do fly from one end of the country to the other daily. It's not perfect, but it's close. I make my own way with my own rules within the laws governing this great country. I do reap the rewards of my labor. Yes, I date a lot of men. Yes, I've slept with most of them. It was the late 60's and early 70's, those glorious years. The strict, anti-woman 1950's were over and we were cutting loose! I was in my middle thirties and loving it. I never looked back to the farm, except on an occasional holiday when Liz and I would reminisce while we sipped wine and enjoyed the simple beauty of peace, quiet and harmony in our own little home.

Now at 35, most men were married, but not all. There were many who also wanted to enjoy the freedom of not marrying. We made good friends. Recently though, I'd really fallen for one guy – London. He'd been part of one of the teams I'd flow with over the past year. He was a co-pilot and quite content with it. We started out talking after a trip while waiting for our co-workers to come off the plane so we could check out together. We usually had dinner together as a team and then headed out on our own for a couple of days off.

During these outings London was usually quiet. I took it upon myself to drag him bit by bit out of his shell. He'd been married 4 years to another stewardess. She'd moved to another airline because we weren't allowed to work together as a married couple. She flew mostly east to New York. Kids weren't in the plan just yet but they'd agreed on two. I'd joke with him about being too old for kids, but his wife was only in her mid-20's so there was still time. London had a kind, jovial manner and was always calm yet calculating.

Maybe we became friends because he was married. I'm really not sure, but we talked endlessly about every little thing. It wasn't long until the rumors started. I'm not sure why men and women can't talk to each other as friends without others assuming sex is involved. When they asked I told them I didn't date within the team, period. When they joked about it, we both blew it off. They rolled their eyes at our denials, but it was true, at least initially, we were only friends.

I was actually on my second month of dating a pilot from United Airlines when he dumped me because I talked about London too much. London switched teams for three months to cover for another co-pilot and it was the longest, hardest, most boring stretch of my adult life. I thought about him every hour of every day. I tried to resist talking about him, but once someone got me started I couldn't seem to stop. I finally just started shopping and getting him little things I thought he'd like. During flights I'd often forget and look in the cockpit expecting to see him. It seemed like an eternity that he was gone. Then, the weekend before he was to start working with the team again, he had a heart attack and was out another 8 weeks.

I sent him cards, but no response. I finally gave up and just checked in with the team to see what they'd heard. Most of those heartless bastards just continued working like nothing had happened. They found another co-pilot to cover the duties and life went on. I however, was miserable for the first time since I'd left the farm. I finally started dating a pilot named Michael. He was kind, pleasant and single. We actually took a weekend and stayed over in Las Vegas. We gambled, danced, partied, made love and collapsed into heap of hotel sheets to sleep. Two days passed then suddenly I'd woken up and no Michael. He'd simply left and left me to pay the hotel bill. Now at the time a single woman checking out of a hotel room in Las Vegas still garnered a few awkward stares and nervous responses. After all, the card had two names on it and I wasn't Mrs. Michael Neem. I felt scandalous, which I found quite exciting and yet unnerving.

When I ran into Michael the next time, I cornered him before he had a chance to run. Apparently after two days he thought I loved him, but when I kept calling him London he left. He claimed I had broken his heart. "After two days?" I said. "You fell in love with me in Las Vegas after two days," I repeated. "Yes, he said, and you stomped all over my heart." He stomped off and I never had the occasion to speak to him about Mrs. Michael Neem which he hadn't mentioned. Whatever. Apparently, I couldn't hide that London was on my mind all the time and everywhere no matter what I was doing, he was there -like a ghost, a stalker but only in my head. London was actually at home with his wife recovering from heart surgery.

London finally returned to work after 12 painfully long weeks. He came back to our team and we all celebrated with cake and ice cream. Our eyes met and he boldly gave me the biggest hug I'd ever had. He looked so good, and was so strong it seemed so bizarre that he'd had a heart attack. He didn't look at all like someone newly recovered from a nearly deadly health episode. "Let's do dinner tonight, 730 pm meet me in the front lobby," he whispered in my ear quietly. "I have missed you so much and we need to catch up," he said. I really didn't want to let go, but I graciously backed away and tried to concentrate on my work. I could hardly wait for dinner and fortunately that day there were no delays, only simple, ordinary flights. As we gathered together at the end of the last flight to head to the hotel, I was nearly beside myself with excitement. We shared a ride over as a group, and then went our separate ways until the morning. Typically, the women would meet around 630 for dinner usually at the hotel. It was frowned upon for us to go outside the hotel unless we absolutely had to. Many girls lived on the free plane meals, but I liked the occasional dinner out to be around other people. The men always met in the lounge and ate between drinks.

At 7:30 I was sitting on the couch in the lobby when London breezed out of the lounge, swept around the lobby and we quickly went outside to a waiting cab. "Take us to the best Italian food in Los Angeles," he said to the cab driver. I loved Italian and he knew it, but it was hard to eat Italian and retain the required weight for the airlines. I'd have to eat carefully. We just stared at each other, unsure who should talk first until finally I blurted out "I missed you so much! It was so boring without you!" He smiled and listened as I continued on a roll, grilling him with questions on his health, how his time off went, his future plans until he finally leaned over, pulled me close and kissed me lightly on the top of the head. He smiled. "Let's say it's was a long and painful 12 weeks. Mostly I slept and ate the food my wife put before me. She took two weeks off to care for me and then the neighbors took turns. She couldn't stand to be home all the time. It all worked out fine and I was catered to like a king," he said with a wide grin.

The cab dropped us off and London paid him for the fare and arranged to have him come back for us in two hours. Two hours for dinner was way too much, I thought to myself but by the time we ate and caught up, two hours was barely enough time. There was so much energy between us that I wasn't really sure what to do. He was like my best friend, advisor and big brother but at the same time our sexual attraction was deafening and hard to ignore. I figured it was just me, but after seeing him again tonight, I didn't believe it was only me any longer. He wanted to kiss me, but he didn't. He wanted to grab a hold of me and dissolve, but we didn't. We continued as friends, for a few more weeks and then one evening we crossed the line and weren't able to back up.

It all started with a lunch on a long weekend we both had off. I went home to visit Liz and do something around the house to help out. We gave each other a new hair color and cut, and a manicure. You can't beat it for quality and money savings, that's for sure. After a full day of girl stuff, Liz was disappointed when I had a date but she tried not to show it. By the time London picked me up at 8pm though, she was already sound asleep on the couch with her hair safely tied up in a scarf so it wouldn't get messed up or transfer any color to the couch. I'd forgotten how fun a girl day was, and made a mental note to try to get home more often.

I was quickly lost in London. From the time he picked me up, to the time I came home after 4am, it was all London. Our friendly movie and ice cream time turned into a movie, walk in the park, ice cream and an accidental kiss which led to a place I'd certainly never been before and still blush when I think about it. It started out as our normal "friends" time. We picked a movie and then decided to walk around the park and take in the stars and quiet evening. We talked and laughed, all very innocently. He put his hand in the curve of my back as we passed other people and eventually it just stayed there as he ordered our ice cream cones and we headed back to his car. He drove to the nearby Monterey beach where Liz and I always sunbathed and used to hit the beach parties. We parked and looked over the ocean as the waves rolled in and out to their own steady rhythm. As I was set to lick the last half of my cone, our lips met. I dropped the cone out the window as we rolled into the back seat and our clothes flew. Months of built up energy poured through both us and we made love that evening until early morning.

We slipped back into our clothes giggling like children and he dropped me off at home and watched me walk all the way into the house, then he slowly drove off . I closed the door quietly and slipped into my bathroom for a quick shower. I had a few scrapes and scratches from the car, and I knew I was going to ache later but it was so worth it. I fell asleep instantly and didn't wake until 10 am the next morning mostly because I smelled fresh coffee and eggs. Liz was cooking breakfast. The long weekend was sheer bliss. Sister time and London time had been had and thoroughly enjoyed. Liz and I spent the rest of the day shopping and then walking the beach in the evening. I knew London and I were more than friends, but I didn't know quite what would happen next. The workday came and Liz dropped me at the airport and actually drove herself to work as a treat. She had new heels and didn't want to walk that morning. New heels are the best!

London, London, London. He was my muse and my nemesis. I struggled to clear my mind and concentrate on work during the week after our stolen evening and weekend meetings. We breezed through months of making love, driving down the coast and stopping for fresh fruits and vegetables at the farm stands. We started staying overnight together both on an occasional weekend and nearly always during the week. We both loved the ocean and the beach so any layover time we got from work we did our best to arrange time near one. I made it home to keep up with Liz at least once a month, so she wouldn't feel abandoned. Not that she really noticed, she was busy either working, walking the beach, or drying flowers. Typically my weekend at home with Liz consisted of flying to, or meeting up in, Reno and gambling. We were both good gamblers and loved the bright lights of the casinos. It was so alive, colorful and loud – it was fun. We'd gamble, and dance into the early hours of the morning and then pass out in the hotel room bed. Neither of us was what you'd call "outdoorsy." We were all about the indoors – shopping, gambling, and dancing. The only part of the outdoors we liked was tanning on the beach and listening to the waves lap the sand.

Liz used to play in the beach volleyball games, but now she just sat back sipped her drink and quietly critiqued the players. "Go join them," I'd say. "No, I'm too old for that," she'd always respond. London made me feel young. I needed Liz to find a similar elixir for youthful energy. I'd give up in the end and we'd both rub on more baby oil, sip our wine and lay out and tan. "Why don't you date anymore?" I asked. "I only date in Reno," she said to me. "Why?" I asked. "Because no one knows me there, and it's fresh and free. I'm over dating," she said ending the conversation with a crusty look and her last word of warning – "and you'd best be careful with that London. You'll get yourself pregnant." "Don't worry about me, I countered, I can take care of myself." Thinking about London made me flush and I rolled over to tan and daydream of London in peace.

We both stayed fit and trim, still at a size 2 and able to pull off the latest fashions in clothes and high heels. Life was good. Liz never asked much about London beyond an occasional and random warning. She wasn't my mother. Bea hadn't talked to me for over a year now since my last drunken rambling. Liz kept me up to date on Bea's life even if I didn't care. She was good, married and working with a successful business. I had to hand it to her, that Bea was a doer. Liz would automatically give me the scoop on any family information as soon as I got home.

You know, I loved my family, I honestly did at least Peter, Bea, and Liz. I did care about the rest, but had no use for my Father and certainly no use for his new wife. Without mother, family wasn't all that interesting to me. I cared and yet I didn't care. If I never saw any of them again, I couldn't have cared less. Liz didn't want to go back to visit but she regularly wrote letters and sent cards for each and every birthday. She signed both our names. Once in awhile, she'd even dial the phone. Bea called her every week and they'd talk for an hour. I never understood what they could possibly talk about that long. I don't know when Liz had the time for all that. She spent nearly as much time at work as I did, minus the travel. Since I'd been staying with London she'd taken up walking the beach and had somehow met a group of 4-5 women who met and walked every weekday morning. She dried flowers and created arrangements. Our house was covered with tight wires a few inches from the ceiling and holding up rows of beautiful bright flowers at varying stages of death. To me it was dreadfully depressing, but Liz found them beautiful. She'd put together dozens of vases and wreaths, all hanging and jammed onto our tiny home's walls.

She'd even sold some to co-workers and was quite proud of that. In my imagination, all I could see was a bank lobby overrun with dried flower arrangements and wreaths in every nook and cranny. Several had wandered into my bedroom and bath uninvited but I let it go.

The next day as I was coming back to reality and we lay sunbathing on the back deck, I noticed a large bump on Liz's back. "What's this?" I asked poking it gently with my fingernail. "I don't know, I have a few," she answered. "I think it's an allergic reaction to one of my plants, " she said. "They move away when you touch them, that's really creepy. You should get those checked," I added. I knew she wouldn't go in and get them checked so I made a mental note to nag her until she saw a doctor. I certainly understood about not wanting to go to a doctor, but those bumps just seemed very odd and they didn't itch like bumps you get with an allergy. They acted almost independent like planets floating in a galaxy.

It just seemed to me that when you visited a doctor you basically paid money for them to tell you to go home and get some rest. I could do that myself. They also insist on knowing every little thing about you. I've felt that either I get condescending looks or they look right through me as if I wasn't there. I didn't go often.

Personally I'd been nauseous for at least a week. I felt bloated nearly all the time and I couldn't keep anything down. I had cut back on my daily glass or two of wine, but that hadn't seemed to help. I laid back down, set the egg timer and lowered my dark glasses for another 15 minutes of sunning on this side. A quick glance around showed no signs of any interesting men, only several families with running and screaming children. The next thing I heard was the sharp shrill of the egg timer going off. "Time to get going," I said without looking around. I tipped my dark glasses off the side of my nose to glance towards Liz, sitting up just enough to make eye contact. I looked right into eyes of a little boy holding a beach ball. He ran back the other way without a word. "Crap," I said to no one as I retied my bikini top around my neck.

Liz was nowhere to be found. It was after 3, so I packed up our things and headed up to the bar. Got a tall glass of white wine from a flirty young bartender and waited for any sign of Liz. "Are you looking for your friend?" he asked as I scanned up and down the beach for any sign of her. "He's a genius," I thought to myself. "Sister," I answered. "Did you see where she went?" I said. He nodded, winked and pointed left. Liz was at the medical tent. I hustled over there, not so easy in high heels and deep sand. She and a doctor were talking. He was gesturing as if he was explaining something. As I approached he handed her a note and a couple of tubes.

Liz smiled back at him with what I knew was her best smile and he gave her a card.

She saw me coming and waved to stop me. I sat down on the closest bench and waited. She finally tipped toed over in bare feet, grinning from ear to ear. He watched her walk until he was distracted by a crying child and its semi-hysterical mother. "What happened? You left me at the beach." I said in what I planned as an angry tone. Liz didn't bite. "Let's go," is all she said and she grabbed a bag from me and headed off to the car. I thought about pitching a fit and staying for the sake of protest, but I was tired and curious. I tossed the rest of my wine into the nearby trash can and hustled to catch up with her. She's so damn bossy, I thought to myself.

After we loaded our stuff and drove two blocks home, she finally said, "Sorry but look," and she took off her cover, turned around and on her back were dozens of oozing lesions covered in balm. "Oh my God, what happened?" I gasped ready to vomit. "He said I needed to come in and have them checked. Probably just sunburn," she said. It surely looked like more than sunburn to me. "He came by after you'd fallen to sleep and insisted I go to the tent. He put the balm on me, which felt much better actually." She said. "Then we got to talking and he gave me a prescription and I have an appointment next Wednesday." "Then I have a date for Friday and he's a doctor!" She was literally grinning from ear to ear. "Well, maybe I should see him too. What kind of doctor is he?" I explained my week of nausea and vomiting while I made our dinner salads and she warmed up tacos that we'd made the day before.

Liz dropped the plates and our eyes met. Her face was completely white. "You okay?" I asked. "You're pregnant," she said as if it was the same as leprosy. Those are the most chilling three words in the dictionary for a single woman who doesn't want children. We sat down and ate our dinner in silence, Liz with her oozing back and me with the possibility of being pregnant. I left the next morning before dawn to head to work. "Call you later. Let me know how your date goes," I wrote on a notepad and left it by the coffee percolator. I added a big smiley face as if I was ten years old. Smiley faces are simply pain twisted sideways.

Night after night I could not sleep. I couldn't go to the airlines doctor or they'd know, everyone would know. I spent my first week totally alone every night feigning illness and trying to figure out what to do. I didn't want to share with anyone and certainly didn't want London to know. He accepted my need for secrecy with concern. He even brought soda and saltine crackers trying to help. I missed two days of flights but finally managed to find a doctor and get tested. Getting the results would take another week so I went back to work. London and I planned a layover in Washington DC for the following weekend.

I went on as usual trying to ignore the nagging in my mind. I could see my Father scolding me in my dreams alongside my mother smiling warmly but with a look of concern. Then, my brothers boxed me up in a crate and shipped me to China. Lois Elizabeth, I heard my mother say in endless dreams night after night. How could you get yourself in this trouble? What did I tell you about saving yourself for marriage? The conversation went on and on in my head night after night. I couldn't focus on planning Washington DC because fear and guilt kept rushing up into my throat and choking my breath. I spent the weekend in sheer agony. Monday came and with it the bad news. The test was positive. I was six weeks pregnant and sick as a dog every single day. All I could envision was my mother spending all her time and energy washing, mending clothes, cleaning and cooking for ten kids, day in and day out.

Mind you, I had nothing against children except I didn't want to have any. I thought I'd been careful, taken the same precautions I had but with London it hadn't worked. "Why couldn't this have happened to Bea?" I asked myself. She wanted kids. "This should not happen to someone who doesn't want them," I said aloud to no one.

Chapter 13

My mind raced trying to come up with a plan. What was I going to do? Maybe Liz could raise it? No, she was just starting to date the doctor and I doubted she'd be interested in switching gears right now. Who is going to care for it during the workday or when I'm away? Thousands of questions without clear answers flooded my brain. I managed to distract myself long enough at work to get through it. Coworkers kept asking me if I was okay because I looked pale and tired. I even cancelled our layover weekend in Washington DC with the excuse that Liz was sick and I needed to be at home. I even volunteered to stay on the ground and work in the office so I could avoid London.

I felt an overwhelming guilt and I couldn't bring myself to face him. I felt betrayed, and simultaneously overwhelmed or horrified by the thoughts that ran through my head. It felt as if they literally ran through my head. I popped aspirin constantly and kept up on the wine. Referring to the baby as an "it" made it seem less personal, but not much. Maybe I could go back and stay with Bea, adopt the baby out, or maybe she'd adopt it? Perhaps I should take the savings I had and move to Los Angeles for a year, work in the airline front office there and then have the baby and adopt it out, no one would know. About that time the doctor's office called. I'd used my work number so they'd reach me and not Liz or worse – London. Maybe I could stay in a hotel half a week and then go home so Liz wouldn't suspect anything? I made an appointment to discuss "planning for a healthy baby" and finished off another glass of wine. Oh God, what was I going to do?

While Lois suffers from her sins and the guilt of not calling me, let's return to Liz. I still can't believe she didn't call me - the good one, the one who loved our nephews and nieces and almost all children. We'll let Lois stew in her mess while we catch up to Liz who was indeed having the time of her life!

Meanwhile, Liz was having what may have been the best years of her life. She'd gotten a new promotion at work and was in charge of the mortgage department. She was the first female director they'd ever had. She enrolled for training two nights a week to learn additional regulations around mortgage loans. She walked nearly five miles a day, some on the beach barefoot and the rest on the sidewalk in heels. She was always careful to use her old heels so as not to scuff her good ones. She frequently walked to and from work diverting in the evenings to the ocean front path to take in the fabulous Monterey sunsets. Finally she'd wander past the flowers and gardens until she arrived home. Scuffed heels were perfect for walking because she still looked good and didn't ruin any good shoes.

Liz met Dr. Berry twice a week for a casual dinner. Then they'd walk hand in hand down the beach. He was impressed by her work and knowledge of finances. He wasn't financially savvy so he enjoyed her banking knowledge and experience. Plus, Liz was a working woman, an attribute also to his preference. To him, she was independent and yet dependent. She let him open doors and buy her dinner, let him be the first to speak when they were out and she didn't talk too much. She was one of the rare women he could talk to and not feel like she only wanted to know how much he made. Liz never asked, not once. Then, of course Liz was beautiful. She was tall even without the six inch heels, had a slim waist and long, elegant legs. Dr. Berry had a hard time concentrating around long legged women in heels. He'd actually had to start running in the mornings to make sure he didn't continue to develop a gut. Liz was so slim and kept in such good shape, he felt compelled to do the same.

Dr. Berry (as he called himself as well) was so proud of graduating medical school that he wanted to repeat the word doctor to himself and others as often as possible. Granted, right now he was just a partner in a small practice and worked mostly on the beach in a medical tent. However, the job paid above average and the scenery wasn't too bad either. Whenever he'd get bored, he'd scan the beach for people sunbathing too long, handing out salve or treating burns, scrapes or jelly fish stings. When he'd come across Liz and Lois sunbathing, he saw Lois fast asleep but covered with a mixture of oil and zinc – she was the careful one. Liz just used oil and figured a burn would fade to a nice tan in just a couple of days. However, typically she didn't burn that badly so when Dr. Berry woke her up he startled her. At first she couldn't tell if the handsome face was part of a dream or reality. The more he went on about burns, she knew it was reality and she was happy about that. He gave her a quick lecture and handed her two tubes of salve.

As she took the salve their eyes met and there was a moment of silence it seemed and then time came rushing back in like it was embarrassed about the delay. She listened intently to the instructions and when he offered, she followed him back to the tent so he could apply it. She forgot all about Lois as she ran to catch up with the doctor.

And so it began, we'll go back to Liz in a bit. Let's go back and catch up with Lois and see how she's faring with her baby decision.

Lois went to her baby appointment ashen grey and wearing a look of heavy foreboding as if she were on her way to her execution. She felt sick, as usual, regardless of what she ate or how much she drank. She was exhausted from sleeping in a hotel room and trying to avoid both Liz and London until she came up with a plan. She'd dialed my number twice at home, but in those days you couldn't tell – there was no messaging service or caller ID. I never knew she called, but I so wish I'd answered the phone. We'll let her explain.

Each time when Bea answered with her cheerful, professional voice, I chickened out and hung up. I couldn't tell her. I dialed Peter's number but hung up while I waited for one of his kids to bring him to the phone. Now here I was watching as this strange doctor told me how to care for myself in order to have a healthy baby. I stared as his mouth moved, but heard hardly anything. I still hadn't decided what to do and I seemed incapable of talking to the few people who could help.

As I drug myself towards the exit, a young nursed whispered in my ear and handed me a slip of paper with a couple of numbers for "alternative services." I took it absentmindedly and smiled. I stopped and picked up a hamburger and a milk shake and headed back to the hotel. I pulled out the slip of paper and stared at the numbers. "What the hell are alternative services?" I said to myself. I finished eating my food and placed the numbers on the table, bathed and fell fast asleep.

Chapter 14

Liz, on the other hand, found herself in love again. She was completely enamored with Dr. Berry and during our weekly phone call she couldn't stop talking about him. I could hardly get a word in. I'll let her tell the story since it's so cute I may vomit.

Since the day I met the doctor by chance on the beach, I've been in love. I've never been so glad to get sunburned. I'd not gone to a doctor since my last car accident, but this time I could hardly wait to make the appointment. The rest of the weekend flew as I herded Lois back to the house to get ready for another week. I was concerned with Lois's drinking as she was always ill, down, and gaining weight. I made a note to talk to her about it when she came back the next time. In my blissful state of total enamoration with Dr. B, I'd forgotten entirely about the pregnancy scare.

I spent the weekend out of the sun, tending to my pots of blooming flowers and mowed the grass – thoroughly enjoying myself. On Monday morning I rose early and took my walk along the beach. I scanned the beach for any new unoccupied seashells. Near the end of my walk, I stumbled upon a huge conch shell! It was unoccupied as well. I carried it back home and left it soaking in the sink. I dressed and left to take on another day at the bank.

I made my follow up appointment with Dr. Berry for Tuesday after work and then made plans to get my hair and nails done Monday evening. I wanted to look perfect, or at least as perfect as possible. I had worked out a system to get the salve on my back but I had used more than I should have. I was certain they were healing fine. I certainly didn't feel anything there and my mirror didn't tell me anything different – they appeared to be healing. I cleaned out my conch shell and laid it out to dry. Dyed my hair to a fresh new blonde and coiffed and wrapped it up in a scarf so the dye wouldn't leak, assuming I could even sleep! I was so excited my heart raced and all my nerves tingled. I imagined Dr. Berry standing close to me, his warmth radiating near me, him sliding his arm around my waist and gently kissing my hair and then my neck.

I imagined him slowly turning me with his arm around my waist to face him, our eyes meeting and him bearing down on me meeting my lips with his, pushing me gently against the wall where his other hand ran up my skirt and then I fell fast asleep deep in dreams until the shrilling of the morning alarm woke me up. I skipped the walk that morning, so I could leave early enough to spend extra time perfecting my makeup and getting my hair right. "Good morning Liz," my boss said his eyes widening as he looked me over. "You look especially radiant today. Special plans?" he asked. "No, just feeling good, and I have an appointment after work." I answered. "Ah, a date then!" he said. "No silly, a doctor's appointment." I said as I grinned and blushed at the same time. He frowned and shook his head saying, "You really need to get out more." "Oh, I plan on it." I added as our daily exchange ended with him walking off shaking his head and my grinning excitedly like a young child surrounded by gifts on Christmas morning.

Now, let's return to our distressed and pregnant Lois. I so wish she talked to me, Bea, as I would have taken them both in. I would have advised her to keep the baby because I truly thought she'd regret the adoption. Here's Lois: I went home for the weekend with the idea I'd tell Liz and get advice. If that didn't work out, I'd call Bea or Peter and not hang up the phone. They loved to give advice and I'm sure they'd delight in my predicament. In hindsight, I should have talked to London. Here I was with no car as Liz always drove. I had calculated my savings and determined that it could hold me over for four months and probably more if I cut back. I should have talked to London, but I just couldn't. He was already married with three small children. I didn't want to be that other, desperate woman. It simply wasn't who I was or am. So I convinced myself that if he'd really cared he'd have tracked me down by now. I'd been working in the office and off the planes for three weeks and nothing – no calls, no notes, nothing. I convinced myself he already knew about the baby and wasn't interested. If he was interested, he certainly never showed it. In the long year that followed, I never heard from him once.

Anyway, I was on my own and an independent woman. I called the alternative numbers the young nurse had given me to see what they had to say. One number took you to Mexico and you stayed in a hospital for two weeks. After the birth, the baby was adopted out for you and you didn't even see it. I didn't like the sound of that.

The other number was a medical office in Los Angeles, and didn't involve much travel and was far less expensive. We won't mince words. The alternative services they offered were abortions. They talked about "eliminating the fetus" as if that meant it wasn't human. I thought about it, it sounded clean and easy. The simplicity of it lingered in my brain. Both numbers claimed I could be back to work in two weeks, no health repercussions whatsoever and no after effects. If I chose the abortion, it was safe and done by a medical doctor. If I chose adoption, they took care of all the paperwork and my name would be anonymous.

I decided to talk to a couple of adoption clinics close to our house in Monterey and just a few blocks down from the airline office. One was quite seedy and told me they'd find the baby a good home in a tropical country, no paperwork necessary. I bolted out of there. The second one offered adoption out within the states and had a place to stay with room, board and medical care. I still wasn't sure, but after another week of debate I'd run out of time. I was starting to show despite the girdles. It was the longest, most stressful week of my life. I'd finally started to be able to keep food down again and so felt quite a bit better. However, it was causing me other pain now. I had constant but brief pulsating pains run through my hands, arms and feet. I had to increase my aspirin and wine just to keep the pain under control.

Despite it all, I couldn't kill it. I simply just could not do it. I understand the need for it, but I still couldn't do it. Weak? Maybe I am weak. Stubborn? Yes, definitely. Abortion was not the answer for me. I chose the adoption place in Monterey. They were confidential and they provided a secret place to stay. They'd bus me to work and back as long as I could work. It would take all the savings I had, plus some. However, I could still check up on Liz even though I'd have to disappear. I got it arranged and for the first time in a month, I slept. Not on my right side, not on my back, certainly not on my stomach but on my left side. Now I just had to figure out how to disappear for the next 8 months without Bea sending out a search party or at least without Liz filing a missing persons report.

It turned out to be easier than I thought it would be. By the weekend, I'd talked to my boss and made arrangements that would allow me to come back to work as soon as possible. I created a story for Liz where I'd met a man and was going to stay with him. She'd be so scandalized and angry she wouldn't miss me for a few months. When I told her that weekend, there was yelling, than tears, and then more yelling. I left with my two packed suitcases and called a cab. I think her excitement over meeting Dr. B. won over in the end. Her parting words were "your room will always be here, and you're getting fat." She'd never asked about the pregnancy and even though the moment presented itself yet again, I couldn't bring myself to tell her. Oh, I so wish it was fat! I kissed her on the cheek, hugged her and headed out the door. The cab was well worth it. I was able to compose myself on the short ride to the complex. As I unloaded my bags in that tiny furnished room, I gazed out the window. They had a small courtyard with a fishing pond in the center surrounded by an acre or two of grass, trees, and a walking path. It looked both peaceful and full of bugs.

From the window, I couldn't see the ocean or the beach. I missed my room at home already! But, it'd be fine, I convinced myself and finished unpacking and storing my suitcases in the closet for the trip back home. I laid down to rest for just a few minutes, and was woken up several hours later by a knock on the door. The welcoming committee came by and handed me a care kit, information on daily activities and when meals were served. I did my best to chat, smile and pretend to be friendly but it was strained to say the least. After they'd left, I turned on the television and fixed my hair and got ready for dinner. I hadn't eaten all day and I certainly didn't want to miss dinner.

As I walked down the path to the dining hall, it all seemed so perfect. The place was a small compound including a security fence and tons of trees. There were 24 apartments total that shared the interior courtyard. They had a guard at both entrances and they checked your ID every time you came and went. Once they got to know me, I passed right on through. I was still working, so I came and went at least twice a day where most of the others stayed put. I really didn't run into that many other women and when I did, I usually wished I hadn't. Either they talked endlessly, or looked so sad it took the air right out of my lungs and I couldn't afford that.

The guards were good too. Any strangers that happened to wander up were quickly and I'd venture to say, roughly, escorted out. It never crossed my mind their reaction to strangers was odd. Although as I learned over the next several months, many of those escorted away were not truly strangers. Rather they were estranged husbands, angry boyfriends, or other family members. Their pain and anger was understandable to me. It would have been nice to know that someone cared enough to get roughed up getting thrown off the grounds. I only saw a couple of times where the cops were called in to assist with an especially difficult extraction.

The next several months were quiet. I continued to work until the last month. I stayed to myself except for the occasional chat as I walked around the pond in the evening or during dinner at a shared table. Making friends was not something I had been good at before, and now with a compound full of pregnant, hormonal women I wasn't interested. Most didn't use their real names and if you can't at least be real what's the point in making friends with someone who can't responsibility for their actions. Others were just despondent, depressed, or overly happy. The extremes were too much for me. So, I stayed pretty much to myself and when I felt lonely in the evenings I'd write a letter to Liz, Bea, and Peter. It made me feel better. Although, making up stories about a fictional man was difficult because I had to remember my lies.

In many ways they spoiled me here. I was warm, safe, happy and able to walk to work. When I got heavier, they gave me transportation back and forth. I almost felt like a princess. I didn't have to cook or clean up outside of my little room. From day one I slept deeply every night because I felt safe. It was wonderful. I guess in a way it was like an assisted living retirement home for the pregnant. I often wondered about Bea. My letters went unanswered and I wasn't up for a phone conversation as yet. I didn't want to risk letting anyone know about my condition. As far as they all knew, I was shacking up with some man who worked for the airlines. Bea and Liz came to mind nearly every day so let's go back and check up with Liz and see how the latest love of her life is going. I'll let Liz take over from here.

Work was long that day, and I watched the clock diligently. Time ticked by so slowly it was aggravating. I didn't want to smudge my makeup, so I continued to smile and try to pass the time as happily as possible. Tick, tick, tick, the noise from the clock sounded extremely loud. The bank was quiet so it was harder to distract myself from clock monitoring. Finally, slowly, 5 pm rolled around and I locked up my desk, dropped the key in my purse and ran for the door.

I walked the short distance to Dr. Berry's office briskly so my cheeks were rosy from the exercise as I entered the office. I sat down giddily, probably the happiest person in a Doctor's office, certainly the happiest I'd been to see a doctor in my lifetime. I twitched nervously, crossing my legs and adjusting my skirt every few seconds. I checked the angle on my left leg to make sure it showed the best side, or at least what I thought was my best side. When the nurse opened the door and called my name, I tried to hide my disappointment. The nurse checked my vitals and weight, commenting heartily on my clothes and we chatted on the best places to shop and find cute clothes that weren't too old or too young. When you're in the late 30's you can't dress too young or people think you're nuts and you can't dress too old – or men won't be attracted to a dowdy stranger dressed like their mother. If they are, that would be a red flag.

Talking to the nurse helped pass the time. I didn't realize I'd have to change into an ugly hospital gown, but I did. The hair and makeup would just have to carry me. My mind raced as I waited and waited, trying not to muss my hair or makeup. I was picking the loose threads on the gown when a tiny, swift door on the door announced his arrival. I couldn't stop myself from smiling and he smiled back, a bit taken back by the energy in the room. He thought to himself how he had seen the first patient in a gown that actually looked attractive. More than attractive, she practically glowed from underneath its drab, safe coloring. But ethics were ethics and regardless of the situation he couldn't date a patient without it damaging his reputation. He'd always told himself not to, and he planned to stick to that. He had steeled his reserve before he'd opened the door, but now that he was in the room with me, he forgot all about ethics.

He smiled at me and did his usual checks. My heart was beating fast, but otherwise I was fine. He checked my back, discreetly looking at the area where the sores had healed well. He told me as much, but I'd have to stay out of the sun and give up the sunbathing. If not, I was inviting skin cancer in especially with what he could see was extensive sun damage already. Dr. B noticed how soft Liz's skin was soft despite the scarring and subtle pock marks left behind. He smiled at me as he told me what I needed to do to avoid aggravating my skin. I nodded and smiled, stuck on every word. I gazed into his eyes and agreed to give up sunbathing

– way too easily. I loved it, but I could give it up for him, that's for sure. I had a tendency to live to please.

As our eyes met again, he felt a significant pause. He couldn't think of what to say next. He was speechless! He couldn't think of the words to say, and finally after a rather awkward pause where Liz looked down at her hands, embarrassed to be caught staring – he blurted out the one question he wasn't supposed to ask – "Would you like to join me for dinner Friday night? I know a small seafood place just up the beach a couple miles. I could pick you up at 7 pm. Do you like seafood?" His mind raced, what if she didn't like seafood and what the hell was he doing? Liz was a patient and he couldn't date a patient. Or could he? I smiled and said yes. That's all he heard the rest of the evening as he jotted down my number and I left with two more tubes of liniment, for what exactly, I wasn't sure since my sores had all healed.

I left a few minutes later and felt like I was floating on air as I walked out of the office, down the hall, and through the parking lot to my car. I had a date! A date with an extremely handsome doctor, I was on cloud nine! I could hardly sleep that evening and it was only Tuesday. There were two and a half very long days to go to Friday evening. First thing I'd do was call for a hair appointment right after work Friday and spend the rest of the week doing my nails and sanding down my elbows. I decided to make a list as soon as I got home so nothing was forgotten.

I arrived home and went to work cleaning the house in a valiant attempt to settle down. I couldn't quit daydreaming, so I wandered from room to room cleaning rather haphazardly. After a few hours, I finally showered and fell fast asleep...still dreaming of Dr. B. Let me dream and you all go catch up with Bea and what's she's up to. Sweet, old Bea.

Chapter 15

Like Liz with Dr. B, I was very much in love with Bryan. He was charming, bright and we enjoyed each other's company whether we were reconstructing the house, redecorating, doing yard work or cleaning the house. Nothing fazed us and it seemed we could do anything together. We even formalized a major vacation plan and for the first time at least in my life, I was going to travel not only within the USA but to Europe and Asia as well. It was hard to fathom now, but I remember being so excited. I had Diana to watch the shop while I was gone. She had proven to be reliable and responsible and had become almost like family, but I trusted her more than family. The only thing I would get behind on was installations that Marvin couldn't do alone, and those were few and far between. Diana's husband agreed to fill in if needed.

Bryan had his real estate partnership and he was always running. But, he planned trips and we worked around them. He tried to make bigger sales, albeit less frequently, and pretty much his pay evened out over the course of the year. He slowed down some from time to time and during those times he took on the majority of the yard and housework which didn't bother me in the least. Real estate sales can be quite flakey with frequent ups and downs but we managed to weather the roller coaster ride with the shop providing the bulk of our everyday income. I still had occasional lingering doubts that rolled slowly through my mind like clouds. Why did he love me? What if he found someone else? What if he went back to his ex-wife, they did have a daughter after all. All those thoughts ran through my mind whenever he seemed to be changing. Change is normal my friends would tell me. I didn't want to rock the boat, so I left it alone. When he was moody, I let him be. When he was feeling lazy and didn't seem inspired to sell homes, I let him be. It typically worked itself out in a week or two.

Our first trip, outside our honeymoon to Estes Park, was 2 years into our marriage. It was to Mazatlan. We stayed in a resort hotel with beach access, lawn chairs, and a swimming pool. I'd never been waited and doted on so much in my life. I was at a loss as to what to do! Bryan laughed at me, his eyes merry and bright. He loved traveling. I'd never realized before, but he really bloomed when he traveled. He spoke some Spanish and enjoyed conversing with the sales people pitching homemade jewelry as well as employees of the hotel. He loved to talk, and he'd talk about anything – but mostly sports. Whatever the sport was, he knew it. Oddly enough he didn't play any sports, but he read, watched, and knew statistics about most of them. While in Mexico, it was soccer. I finally had to abandon him a few times and go off to the market to shop alone.

I found several painted tree bark pictures that were colorful and unique. Mostly animals of all varieties and all colors, but they always had orange in some shade – my favorite. I found brilliant colored glass bottles, sun sculptures as well as pots and pans. Bryan couldn't believe what I could buy at a market in Mexico, but I found a lot to take back. He flinched at the cost of the shipment, but otherwise he smiled. It was romantic, our room was clean and the windows open – as in there was no glass. You had to be quiet, or at least I had to be quiet, but we made love under the sun, the moon and the stars. It was beautiful and relaxing and we were closer than ever. Spending so much time together seemed perfect and we breezed through each day. I was happy to go home at the end of the week, but at the same time I was sad. I hoped we could continue the romance again back home – without the tropical sun or the incredible sunsets.

Six months later, we took part in a two week cruise to the Caribbean, then a week around Hawaii, and then finally a 4 day cruise to Alaska. In the following years, we visited London, Frankfurt, Florence, Monaco, Denmark and Morocco. The sunsets and colorful blend of tastes, smells and visual art was superb. I mailed back package after package. Poor Diana had to manage the shop and pile up my boxes. I had so much fun finding all my treasures and I grew more excited to open them up in the shop and see what I could match them up with for draperies and carpets. Colors and patterns rolled through my head like paint in a circular bowl and my mind swirled continuously with ideas.

It was both exhausting and invigorating. I loved traveling but I also loved my home more. The first four years were fun, but as we moved into the fifth year I found myself losing the passion to pack and get on a plane. Bryan agreed to whittle down to three trips a year, which was more affordable as we paid off each trip once we got back home. We were in the peak of our earning life and enjoying the heck out of it. My shop's storeroom was bursting with boxes from all over the world and it took me months to unpack and reassemble it all into decorating ideas and themes. My customers loved it – well, most of them did. Some didn't approve of anything foreign, even if it was just an unusual color or theme.

Bryan and I were clicking on all cylinders and even had started discussing when to have children. I let him bring it up because I'd never been in much of a hurry. Having so many brothers and sisters will do that to you. I'm not sure it was that, or the hard farm work, but when I thought of having children I felt tired. Yet, as the years went by and my small nieces and nephews visited us on the occasional weekend, I started to change my mind. One can say it was the biological clock or just a normal yearning for children, but the bug bit me at 38 and I wanted to have children. We decided to try and have at least two, preferably one of each. In order to prepare, Bryan brought home my first indoor pet – a golden colored cocker spaniel puppy.

She was my constant companion at home and work. Marvin built a little pen for her inside the workshop and we all took turns taking her outside for short walks. I fell head over heels for that dog. We settled on the name Ginger after a couple weeks of discussion and eventual compromise. I was finding one compromised frequently in a marriage– it's just the way people get along. I don't know if it's really due to marriage, or just a close relationship between two people. Either way you have to work out differences of style, opinions, thoughts, deeds and any number of other things too numerous to mention. Bryan and I usually ended up in heated discussions for several days before we made a decision and Ginger's name was no different.

We kept trying but no pregnancy. I got advice from my sister-in-law Evelyn, on things to try, but nothing seemed to work. In the first year, we did learn a lot about taking care of Ginger. All kidding aside, it was truly a good way to plan for children. Ginger needed walked, she had vet appointments, toys and she had to be disciplined and given a lot of attention. The one thing she did love was playing fetch. She'd fetch a ball much longer than anyone could throw it. Back and forth, back and forth endlessly she rarely got tired and you had to actually stop and put the ball away. Lots of good life lessons for raising kids.

My shop was extremely successful and I now had four employees and good ones too. Bryan had his real estate partnership and his income came and went. During the high times we planned our travel. During the down times, he spent time painting the house, doing the lawn, and maintaining the dozen or so roses he'd planted. Personally, I had no interest in tending to flowers, yards, grass, or trees. All I really wanted to do with a house was decorate it.

Our three trips a year were long and we'd be gone at least three weeks each time. It'd been hard at first. Ginger didn't like to be alone long, let alone for three weeks. Marvin graciously agreed to take care of her when we went away and it went well. She loved Marvin more than she loved either Bryan or I. However, in all honesty Ginger loved most anyone who liked dogs. She loved most of the nieces and nephews or at least those who would throw a ball for her. We could go on trips without worrying about our work or the dog and Marvin checked on the house as well. I'm not sure what I would have ever done without Marvin. He was truly the best right hand man a business owner could have.

Our first trip for the year was to Spain. We went back and forth on tour buses and trains. Spain has beautiful markets, wonderful food and generally friendly people. I enjoyed the trips and during these weeks we focused on each other more than ever. After all, there were fewer distractions.

We didn't have to work or worry about fixing something in the house. We could sleep in, sip wine all day and eat to our hearts content. When I started gaining weight I hoped it was pregnancy, but it wasn't. I cut back, skipped meals but still gained weight. I don't know if I got used to eating more food while traveling, and couldn't cut back when I got home or what. I did the same things I always had, but had gained at least 50 lbs since we'd married. Bryan didn't mind, he'd gained 50 lbs. too. We made a pact to start exercising. Maybe as one approaches 40, excess weight just sticks to you like mosquitoes on a warm, moist evening.

Two years passed and no pregnancy. Bryan wanted me to get checked. I'm not sure why but he'd never gone to a doctor for any reason so he figured since I had, it'd be easier if I went first. Yeah, right he just hoped it was my problem so he didn't have to go. I made an appointment with my regular doctor where we discussed options that I didn't want to consider yet. When I continued to complain, he sent me to a fertility specialist for testing. I went through the most embarrassing tests I'd never known existed and found out that I couldn't have children. Believe it or not, I was already in menopause at 40! My weight gain was the result of menopause, well that and eating too much. When you're body decides it's slowing down, it's slowing down like it or not and I didn't like it at all. It made me start thinking about Bryan and I.

At what point do you realize you're drifting apart? I mean our vacations were wonderful each and every time, but it's almost like we lost the romance as soon as we got home. Bryan started on the house and yard and I went to work. More and more Bryan preferred to stay home and do projects rather than go to work. His sales were way down and his income was getting smaller and less frequent.

On one hand, I didn't mind him doing the house and yard work. I certainly wasn't interested in it and the shop took all my energy and time. But, on the other hand, it struck me as, well, unmanly or unhusbandly. Granted we could make it on the shop together, with scaled back vacations but I found it irritating me more and more as time went on. When I brought it up he'd shrug it off and tell me he was just in a sales slump and he'd sign up for a training class or seminar. As I often did, I brought it up with Diana and Marvin at the shop. They were closer than family to me. They were my right and left hand employees and we truly cared for each other as friends. Marvin told me the same thing he'd been telling me since he met Bryan - ditch him. Marvin was slightly older than I, but certainly not my father's age. However, he represented a father figure to me. I had a hard time telling if it was strictly a male issue between dominant types or a real problem with Bryan. A problem I hadn't even glimpsed in the previous eight years of our marriage. Diana listened, nodded and we discussed ways to find out what he was doing on the sly. She had a friend who investigated businesses and executed financial audits for third parties. She thought he could get help to look up what Bryan's business was up to.

A few months went by with nothing unusual occurring outside of my starting to walk Ginger for a few miles every day. I was proud of my consistent walking and it was helping me to steady my weight without feeling like I was starving. Bryan accompanied Ginger and I most evenings and I personally found it rewarding and pleasant because it gave us time to talk. It seemed to free us up for discussions with more depth. Frequently we even held hands like teenagers and kissed in the street. It brought some fun back into our relationship again. We were more than just work, home and Ginger. However, despite the relaxing demeanor and the in-depth discussions, Bryan never brought up work, money or anything else outside the ordinary. Despite the hints that he was treating me as the fool, for some reason I trusted him anyway and went along as usual, enjoying the normalcy, tenderness and quiet.

Meanwhile at the shop, we were heading into the holiday season and another Halloween was quickly approaching. Like clockwork we worked on changing the display windows for the fall season. It usually took us late into a couple of evenings to complete, do inventory and reset the decorative items, placing last season's leftovers in the bargain bin. The bargain bin was Diana's idea and it was successful in two ways. First it brought in new people on a regular basis who just checked out the bin. If we were lucky, they actually looked around and ended up buying a pillow or something small. Second, the bargain bin "collectors" as I called them sometimes turned into major or regular clientele.

On the evening before Halloween, Diana and I were finishing up the final window when she motioned to me to speak in private. "We need to talk after everyone leaves. I got information for you back from my friend," she whispered as if it were a state secret. My stomach immediately twisted and burned. Somewhere in my subconscious I knew there was something up with Bryan and now I was afraid of what it was. Peter and Marvin never liked him and they barely made a secret of it. I thought that had been just male posturing but maybe I was wrong. I concentrated just long enough to finish the display and barely refrained from rushing everyone home. Once we were alone, I grabbed a candy bar from the vending machine and poured the last of the coffee into my cup. We sat down in my office and Diana twisted her hands in her lap while I arranged myself for bad news.

Her tone had immediately signaled bad news to me and in her face I saw the same reaction. I felt like I was leading the meeting of a secret society, sipping my coffee and breaking off pieces of my snickers bar. "So…what did you find out?" I said. She looked at me with sad and nervous eyes, still twisting her hands. "Relax," I said, "whatever it is, you didn't do it." She gave me a look of relief and stared at me for few more seconds before she continued. "Bryan's company closed its books over a year ago and sold to an undisclosed buyer for a solid profit," she said. I sipped my coffee as I listened and considered what she was telling me. "Bryan has the money stored in a local account in his name, but never seems to use any of it. He has it in savings bonds," she added. So, I thought to myself where was he going when he was pretending to go to the office? Why hadn't he told me and mostly why hadn't we discussed it?

Thankfully, that was it and Diana stopped talking and waited to see what I had to say. Like schoolgirls, we devised a plan for her husband to follow Bryan and see where he went when he told me he was at the office. I paid the house bills, but he didn't ask me for spending money and he spent a bit here and there for hardware, parts and who knows what else. If he wasn't taking it from the account with the money for the sale of his business, or more correctly, our business, where was he getting spending money? I had Ginger that day because he was "working." She stared at me, it was her usual time to go home and walk. "Thank you, Diana," I said. "I really do appreciate the information, but now I don't know what exactly to do with it. If we can find out where he's going when he's "working" then I guess we'll find out more." She looked at me wide-eyed and asked," you don't think he's cheating on you do you?" "Let's not jump to conclusions just yet," I said calmly. Ginger whimpered again and I cleaned up my desk and shuffled Diana out the door and off towards home. We agreed she'd let me know when she'd found out where he was going. I didn't really know if I was hurt or just curious. I wasn't exactly sure how I should feel or how I felt. After I walked Ginger, I picked up fried chicken with the fixins' which was Bryan's favorite, and headed home.

I could have been a Barbie doll I was that plastic. I didn't let on about anything for the next several months as I discovered the man I married wasn't exactly who I thought he was. But, don't get carried away, it wasn't nearly as exciting as it may sound. In the meantime, we went on our second trip of the year and I was still pretending to digest what to do since I couldn't have children. Bryan wanted to adopt, he already had a daughter so it wasn't as big a deal to him. I had my nieces and nephews who I saw at least once a month or more, so I wasn't sure it was a big deal for me either. Part of me was just sad. Sad, or just quiet – it really didn't have much of a response. It was almost like that part had died and its dreams with it, without my even realizing it. And now, that I knew Bryan wasn't exactly who I thought he was, the question was ultimately answered even if he didn't know it yet. I'd not be adopting children with a man who hid money and outright lied to me daily saying he was "off to the office." I started insisting on taking Ginger every day because I knew at least she was loyal and I didn't want her exposed to anything nasty if I could help it. I had to let him keep her a few days just to avoid suspicion. After all, I suppose she was his dog too and I knew he doted on her endlessly.

Bit by bit more information trickled in as if we were police detectives in a murder investigation, or better yet, a high dollar white-collar crime. The pieces of information gathered really didn't seem like much. Diana's husband followed Bryan every couple days for several months. He prided himself on being a fan of Sherlock Holmes and so thought himself a bit of a detective. On one day, Bryan hung out playing golf with his former business associates all still reporting to their shared real estate office. Another day, Bryan did some plumbing work at a house I didn't know and did a bit of electrical work at another. He spent a few weeks painting and several more mowing lawns, tending gardens, and trimming trees. People gave him cash at the end of the day and he shoved it in his right front pocket.

The three of us decided he was basically doing handyman work around town. It couldn't pay as much as being a realtor I presumed, but it answered where he got his spending money. The odd thing was, well, one of the odd things was, he never seemed to put the money anywhere. He had to have it somewhere, unless he spent it as soon as he got it, but not so soon that it gave rise to my suspicions.

It all seemed rather boringly normal, so I suspended the investigation and we entertained ourselves by redecorating Diana's place with what we could scrape together to fit her budget. It proved to be the creative juice I needed to step back and just let life go on its way while I defended my corner of it. After we got done with Diana's place, the holidays started gearing up and we didn't start on Marvin's until the following spring when business seemed to slow down until summer arrived.

It was after we went back and added a nursery to Diana's place that I noticed a cool wind had started blowing through my hair. I often thought someone was there, but only a cool breeze and nothing else. It was eerie, as if someone was brushing past me just enough to move my hair or clothes but was never actually there. I decided it was a sign to contact the girls and see how they were holding up. It was just before Christmas. Lois had sent a card for Thanksgiving, but no return address or number so I'd talked with Liz. It seemed rather odd and unbelievable to me that Liz didn't know where Lois was or even how she was. Liz was caught up and fully engrossed in her work and Dr. B. They'd gotten engaged at Thanksgiving – news I would have like to have known earlier. They were planning a June wedding. I instantly got excited and started jabbering about helping her find a venue, setting up the guest list, and making a list of decorations we'd need and in what exact colors. I got carried away before I could stop myself. Liz finally interrupted me after letting me go on much longer than usual. "Bea. Bea! Bea", she said louder until I heard her.

"My wedding is in California, by the beach, just the family members that can make it, Lois, and a few friends. It will be less than 20 people, small and informal. No need for any extra decorating," she said. I protested in vain, but she stayed her course on a dull, quiet wedding amongst close family and friends. I did promise to attend. Now it was nearly March and I hadn't heard from either of them. Liz answered right away in a happy, chipper voice I hadn't heard in years. Liz was still quite content and still planned on a small, quiet wedding. She was radiantly happy and unusually congenial. Granted it wasn't much different than her usual demeanor, but it was. She had always been pleasant, but reserved. She could get cranky fast though as well.

Chapter 16

I didn't discuss my problem with Bryan with Liz at the time because I didn't want to disturb the peace. We talked for over an hour on pleasant generalities. Liz seemed confident Lois would come to her senses and come home eventually. She and Dr. B had plans to buy the same house they'd been living in. Liz was excited to exit the "renter" world and actually own her little house on the beach. I promised to stay a bit and help her decorate after the wedding. She agreed, but I'm certain only because she wanted off the phone. Dr. B had arrived home and she couldn't miss a second of his time. I hung up the phone and was surrounded by a warm feeling of complete peace. I called her every week on Sunday to get that feeling back.

The cold breeze I felt seemed to be getting stronger and colder. Bryan and I were still muddling along. I decided to confront him after the holidays, in January when we traditionally planned out that years travels. The weekend before Christmas Bryan brought down a fresh pine tree from the mountains. It took nearly 8 hours to find one, cut it and drag it back to his truck. It was four feet too tall for our ceiling, so he cussed and moaned as he cut and re-cut the trunk until it fit. To his credit, when he got the lights on and hung our growing collection of Christmas bulbs, it became an inspiring spectacle of beauty.

Over the Christmas holiday, one of my adult nieces stayed with us. I frequently visited her family whenever I traveled to Denver for materials. I couldn't believe she would be off to college that spring. She was starting early in the spring semester instead of the typical fall. The holiday was busy, but fun. Ginger loved the company, someone else to throw her balls, chase her around and pick up her toys.

As the holidays closed down, as it did every year, it seemed colder and sadder in January. New budgets had to be enforced and adhered to and spending ceased. Business had been slowing down a bit as more competition with cheaper products started to move into town. I had to figure out an approach to the new challenges coming. Larger retailers were opening stores in Greeley and they had less expensive, imported options. They couldn't match our quality, but they certainly could beat our price.

I was in the midst of a business strategy session with Diana and Marvin when the phone rang. It was my brother Peter. "Hey kiddo," he said. "When can you come up here and visit?" He sounded odd, so I just listened. "Dad died yesterday," he blurted out. "He was only 68." Now I knew why I'd felt that cold wind. "Services are next Wednesday, 10 am at the Lutheran church. I hope you can make it." Peter had a hard time getting all the words out and shortly I heard his wife Evelyn's voice in the background. She took the phone. "Bea? You still there," she asked. "Yes, I am," I answered quietly. "Sorry, Peter's still quite upset. Grace didn't tell us until late yesterday when Peter happened to call at his usual weekly time to see if Papa wanted to go to town or needed anything." She rattled on about the retirement complex they lived in for a few minutes. At the end, all I comprehended was her promise to call me with the exact service details. I hung up the phone and let out one large, long sigh. Diana & Marvin just stared. "We're so sorry Bea," they both said as they stared down thoughtfully at the balance sheets before them.

No matter what, who it was, death is always awkward. No one really knows what to say or do. The good people start doing something, anything. "We can finish another time," Marvin said uncertainly. "No, no let's just finish this. I need to have this finished and I can deal with my Father later." We continued on in odd bursts and starts for a while, but got our flow back relatively quickly. We knew our options, discussed a few initial plans of attack and then each of us went home with assignments to research and bring back a list of pros vs. cons and expected results. It felt so good to finish that discussion, and put off even thinking about my Father until I got home.

When I got home, Bryan already knew. Peter had apparently been dialing everyone he could get a hold of. He wasn't going to deal well with this at all. My heart filled with both dread and sadness for Peter. Peter was always Father's right hand man. Peter was capable and he had always been the favorite, golden child.

For me, I honestly felt nothing for my Father. It was sad but I wasn't upset. As a female child he'd never spent time with us. During a meal he may have praised a dish we'd made or a pie we'd baked, but usually not. Anything Father had to say generally came through our mother. He and Grace had come to my wedding for a bit but were gone as soon as Peter had a chance to drive them home. He'd given me the only gift he'd ever given me – my mother's old Bible. "She'd want you to have this," was all he'd said. It was large, dusty and full of page markers and dried flowers. I was sad now and cried for hours, for mother. I dug that Bible out and read it the whole weekend and by Monday I was ready. Right on time, Evelyn called to give me details. Liz also called to say she wasn't coming. She told me instead of Peter. We all loved Peter, he was both our father figure and big brother wrapped into one and very hard to turn down or disappoint. One simply couldn't do it easily, at least not directly.

"What about Lois," I asked, mostly out of habit as I assume Liz would answer for them both. "Beats me," she answered rather curtly. "I've left her messages at work but she never calls me back. I've no idea what she's doing and I

assume she doesn't want to be bothered with us," Liz said
flatly. "Where do they live, or do you know his last name?"
"Maybe I can look them up," I said overly kindly to shift her
mood to back to the happy and peaceful she'd been before I
mentioned Lois. What had these two done to each other? We
said our goodbyes and I promised to sign her name to my
card for Peter. I hung up the phone as a chill caused the hair
on the back of my neck to stand up. Even as we approached
middle age when a woman got pregnant, she did one of two
things in my day: 1) disappeared for a year and then
suddenly returned as if she'd never been gone, or 2) got
married suddenly in Las Vegas or at the county courthouse.

As close as those two were I couldn't imagine why Lois
may have been keeping Liz in the dark. There was one way
to find out – Diana's husband. I'd have him find her for me.
After all she had a right to know her father died, although it
was unlikely she'd care. I was already watching Bryan, why
not Lois too? I just hoped she hadn't done anything stupid or
dangerous. Diana's husband tried for a month to find Lois
without any luck. He did find an address but was unable to
access the property without getting accosted by security
guards. So, I mailed Lois a card with a short letter so at least
she'd know Father had passed.

In the meantime, I'd taken up redecorating my home one
room at a time, as a value added distraction to keep me from
worrying about what Bryan was up to. He didn't seem to act

any different except he wanted to travel more and I wanted to stay home. I'd put off confronting him until after the holidays and here it was already the middle of February. Father's death gave me an excuse to forgo taking any action out of the ordinary with Bryan now. Lois's assumed situation would come up next. If we could get through these events then I'd confront him and find out what he was up to and put it behind me. Meanwhile, we continued on like nothing had changed and I stalled on travel while he looked up more places to go.

Father's service came and went. The pews were filled with all the local farmers who had worked with he and Peter along with their wives and families. It was nightmarish watching the pain in Peter's face. I was the only daughter who showed up, probably because I was the only one who still lived close.

Father's eulogy was given by the pastor at the local Lutheran church where he attended every Christmas and Easter. Other men spoke dearly of a man I didn't even know. I was entranced by the vast differences in our perspectives. Grace played the widow poorly. She was covered from head to foot in black, even including a veil. I never saw her shoulders shake from sobbing or use a Kleenex to wipe away tears. She just sat like a stone as he was buried and again at the reception – or whatever you call that time after the burial where everyone shows up for beverages and snacks. It was quiet, somber and painful until the last person left and I stayed behind and helped clean up the mess.

Chapter 17

Before I knew it, it was June and I found myself in California standing with about a dozen people watching as a bride and groom started their lives together. Liz and Dr. B stood facing the ocean in the sand, she in 6-inch white satin heels and a short gown that showed her exceptional legs and tiny figure. It was a tight, plain dress paired with a veil stitched with tiny blue flowers. She'd had her hair frosted and swirled in a bun atop her head. Her bun was held by the same white satin ribbon and tiny blue flowers. Dr. B was in a black satin suit with a bright blue tie. They looked stunning in the evening sunset saying their vows while the breeze blew and the tide came in. Lois was there in a short blue mini skirt and heels that matched Liz's only the hue was slightly different. Her hair was also frosted blonde and piled up on her head with a blue satin ribbon. They'd made up, I gathered. I hadn't gotten a chance to catch up with either of them recently aside from helping get the bench tent set up and doing some final touches. It seemed like we called each other once a week for a few months and then for some reason skipped several months or even a year. Why we continued to do that, I've no idea. I guess we weren't very consistent.

It was a simple and beautiful wedding. Liz and Dr. B had several friends who all congratulated them and helped pick up all the decorations from the beach after the short ceremony. They had the reception at their newly purchased beachfront home. Simple finger foods, all with a seafood theme graced several small tables set with white or blue satin tablecloths and vases of tiny blue California blue bells. They had set up a small temporary dance floor in the back yard and strung white Christmas lights from one end to the other. It was quite a sight on a warm, southern California evening. The party lasted until the wee hours of the morning, but it was never loud. The music was soft, the food was good and most of the people just chatted and danced until they left one by one. I hadn't tasted so many varieties of seafood and vegetables in my life. The dessert was bowls of fresh cut fruit and real whipped cream. The wedding cake was 7 tiers of angel food and fresh blueberries pressed between layers of light, sweet cream. It was held together with a very thin layer of white icing. It was delicious and I was not much of a blueberry fan.

Lois and I drove Liz and Dr. B to the airport as they were headed for their honeymoon in Hawaii. They both looked tired and yet still radiant. He was certainly charming with an authentic kindness that I'd never experienced in a doctor. I didn't have much time to talk with him but hoped we'd have a chance again before they took off, but that was wishful thinking. Liz never left his side except to use the bathroom, and the time never seemed right.

Chapter 18

Liz and Dr. B were off to Hawaii, still in pure bliss and I'm guessing glad to finally be alone again. Good for them I say, good for them because I was stuck with Lois. After the airport drop-off of the honeymooners, Lois and I headed back to their home and changed into comfortable clothes. I poured myself a large glass of ice water and turned on the TV. Lois joined me after a few minutes. An eerie tension hung in the air between us like a beaded curtain. I tried to start a conversation about politics, then the weather, but Lois just gave me that airline stewardess plastic smile and a short, non-descript answer. I tried to push a button, any button but no real response just the same genial answer. Finally, we said "good night" switched off the TV and headed for bed.

I didn't have to go far since I was sleeping on the couch. Liz had a fancy sleeper sofa and it was beautiful, but not comfortable. Lois helped me roll it out and make it up – not that you needed more than a sheet in Monterey. Monterey was always pleasantly warm. As I was asking myself why I'd decided to stay an extra day, Lois said, "Let's walk down to the beach tomorrow and go shopping. There's some nice little stores there with some fashionable clothes, scarves – liven up your closet." I let that go and said, "Sure, that'd be wonderful." I figured I could at least distract myself with shopping and kill a day before I headed home. I don't recall ever being so tense and miserable since I'd left the farm. I wished Bryan had come along, but he didn't much care for southern California.

Sunday morning came slowly. It was after 10am by the time we'd bathed, dressed, and had a cup of coffee. "I'll take you to our favorite donut shop for breakfast, so you won't want to fill up just yet," she said. "Sounds fantastic," I said with honest enthusiasm and we headed down the street. I was dressed in my shorts and flat sandals and Lois in a bright red mini skirt, skimpy yellow top, red floppy sun hat, and bright, yellow heels. It never ceased to amaze me how much they'd walk in those heels. I'm certain that we looked like a mismatched pair. I could barely see the little girl in Lois who'd chased toads and splashed around the creek so many years ago.

We got to the donut shop and Lois automatically moved to a booth in the back facing the beach. The booth was white with random red polka dots on the seats and walls with a black & white checkerboard floor. Lois told me to sit as she headed to the counter. After a few minutes, she returned with two large raspberry jelly filled donuts, glazed and dusted lightly with powdered sugar as well as two large coffees. I was hungry enough to swallow the whole thing at once, but I restrained myself. It was so good, fresh, and soft. Aside from the jelly, it tasted just like the greble our Mother used to make every week, typically on Sundays. I closed my eyes and sighed for a moment. Lois laughed and said, "Remind you of something? Mother's greble?"

We reminisced for a few sips of coffee. Finally, I had at least made a connection with Lois. We chatted until the lunch crowd starting wandering in and then we headed out. We spent the bulk of the afternoon browsing through one store after another. Lois bought two shirts to switch out with her red skirt and three pairs of pumps in white, lime green and orange. It was pleasant walking around and taking in the scenery and shopping. I found a peach scarf with tiny medallions sewn into it that I couldn't live without and a necklace made of tiny carved wooden elephants. They would do to "liven up" my outfits as Lois would say. She'd have me in a hot pink mini skirt with a fluffy blouse and pink heels – but such was not my style. I don't have a mini-skirt shape or the wherewithal to make sure I wasn't flashing everyone when I sat down or bent over or, well, you get the picture.

We had a late afternoon lunch and headed back. I had to put together my suitcase and call a cab to get to the airport. Lois was not comfortable driving and to tell you the truth, I wasn't comfortable with her driving either. I had my suitcase and handbag packed and ready to go in just a few minutes. While we waited for the cab over a coke, Lois fidgeted in her chair and a light sweat covered her forehead. "Are you okay?" I asked. "Yes, I have to tell you something or I need to tell you something but I'm not good at it and I'm not sure where to start," she said. "I tried to call you, but I hung up every time you answered the phone, I don't know why I couldn't tell you. I had a baby girl last year and gave her up for adoption. Liz doesn't know either, or doesn't remember. It happened quickly and at a bad time, but I couldn't raise it and I didn't want to kill it, so I found a local place and had her adopted. They took care of everything. I don't know why I couldn't tell you, but I couldn't," she said. She said it all so quickly my mind was reeling trying to catch up. I had a suspicion, but now it was confirmed. The taxi honked his arrival, and I gathered up my things. My eyes filled with tears and I had nothing to say. I thought I had plenty to say, but nothing came out – I just wanted to cry. I gave her a quick hug and ran out the door, suitcase and purse flying behind me.

"I'll call you later when I get home," I said before I shut the door. One of the most poignant memories I have of Lois is her standing at that door watching me run with my bags to the taxi. I hadn't looked at her, I hadn't scolded her, I just ran with tears in my eyes. She looked tiny and small and hard to me then. In recollection, it was probably the best for the baby girl to get adopted. But, now I knew she was out there, somewhere, and I'd never know her. I choked back tears all the way home and broke down when Bryan picked me up. I told him the story between waves of tears.

For all his faults, Bryan knew when to just be there and for once he was just there, quietly comforting me. I had nightmares for weeks and I don't know why. But Bryan's kindness and caring kept me from confronting him about his real estate business. It just never seemed to be the right time. I decided not to return to California, next time they'd have to come home to Greeley.

Almost a month later, I was immersed in getting the store set up for the next couple of seasons. Business was brisk. Ginger and I still walked and we were up to about 3 miles a day. She kept me company at work and at home. It was fine by me. We met Peter for lunch every couple of weeks to keep up with the family and what was happening at the farm. Occasionally on a Sunday I'd even drive the 40 minutes out there from town. Now that I was married, it was easier to see them all and Bryan fit right in. He never stopped talking which was great in this crowd. He could keep right up with them.

I got to know a few of my nieces and nephews and brought them Sweet Tarts on the Sundays I came out. It was something they just didn't get much of and they loved it. They'd be waiting at the door for me when I pulled into Peter's place and they'd all spill out the door politely trying to wait and see if I had brought them candy.

I phoned Lois when I got home, but she never answered. It was a couple months before I heard from either Lois or

Liz. Liz sent thank you cards for her gifts, hand written and well phrased. She'd even sent the whole family a wedding picture. Liz called one Sunday evening when I'd just gotten home. "So, she told you about the baby?" "Yes, she did." I answered flatly. "I didn't know either, not one word, not one question, not one conversation," Liz said. "I can't believe she didn't tell either of us." That's where we left it and then we discussed their honeymoon trip to Hawaii and the usual day-to-day things of life. I'd thought she'd change careers and help Dr. B out with his office, but she didn't, she stuck with the mortgage banking. After all she'd tell me, they had to have some space apart. Then we circled back and discussed Lois. She was back in San Diego in her own apartment and dating a retired pilot she'd met in the office. He was a widower with a couple of grown children. They came down every so often to visit and catch up. Liz and Dr. B had purchased that little house by the beach in Monterey the two of them had lived in for so long. We discussed decorating, cleaning and all those types of things. I enjoyed her conversations and general sense of happiness.

My own personal life had taken a turn for the worse. I had needed to confront Bryan but I'd avoided it for one reason or another for several years. Bryan liked to travel and we'd basically started traveling separately when I wasn't up for where he was going. I was into enjoying my own space and weary of the hustle and bustle of travel. I'd even taken up golfing at the course downtown with some friends and business associates. I'd started to hear rumors, little hints dropped during casual conversations about Bryan. Friends looked down or looked away when the subject came up. Diana and Marvin had even grown colder on Bryan. Anytime I mentioned him, they'd mumble and turn away in disgust.

I never got to confront him personally, just in court. He wasn't able to tell me either but eventually he quit coming home. He'd drop off dog food and toys for Ginger and then pretty soon, nothing. I found him at the airport taking off on a trip to Mexico with his girlfriend, a young nurse he'd met doing whatever it was he had been doing. I didn't yell, I didn't scream I self-served him divorce papers. I probably should have yelled and screamed because what I thought would be an easy process turned ugly fast. My lawyer and his went to war. It was a very trying couple of years. It took nearly two years for the divorce to be finalized and all we had owned together divided up and sold. My business faltered and swayed but Marvin and Diana helped me keep it going. Even as busy as we were, small town people were not comfortable with divorce. My business nose-dived and without Marvin and Diana it surely would have failed.

Chapter 19

The house in the country club sold quickly and I found a similar one a few miles away in a new neighborhood. It had a huge basement with two bedrooms and a full bath, lots of storage. I could, if I needed to, move my business there. I couldn't have run a business in my home in the country club, but I could here. It was a smaller house, no doubt, but still spacious enough for myself and Ginger. Over my dead body would Bryan get Ginger. I think Bryan made out better in the divorce, and after a year of sending him checks from the shop dividends, I decided to sell it instead and get the deadbeat off my payroll for good. Of course, he got his final cut and then it was finally over. Diana and her husband bought the business and Marvin and I did drapes and upholstery for her from my basement. Diana had the energy to change and adapt to the constant invasion of large retailers and import competition. I preferred to do the simpler, customizations I enjoyed. I had saved quite a bit over the years and even after the divorce I was able to reduce my hours. I'm not sure how it happened, but I still seemed to be busy even though I was working half as much.

Liz and Dr. B even came out to Greeley, met the family in person and helped me move into my new home. Well, none of us really moved anything –we watched Marvin direct the movers with the boxes and equipment and get it all set up. We had a big Sunday fourth of July party at the farm and they were able to come. Peter loved Dr B. Peter had really slowed down in the past few years. His sons did the majority of the actual farm work as Peter managed the business end. He seemed restless and nervous even though he should have been happy. The farm was worth over 15 million dollars in land value alone. He'd turned a family farm into a coop of farms with over 8000 acres. Dr. B finally got him to loosen up that evening and after a few too many beers he spilled the beans. He'd bought a Daytime's donut franchise and was scheduled to get it open in the next 6 months.

We all just sat and stared at him for a few moments until Dr. B broke the silence with, "I love donuts!" I just blinked. "Why donuts?" we all asked at once. It wasn't like he sold the farm for a Daytime's franchise but it was a significant investment in a chain restaurant still not warmly accepted in the small town of Greeley. "Mother made the best donuts, and Daytime's is willing to let me customize my offerings to include both their recipes and ours. My sons and their families are ready to take over the farming business and frankly I'm bored," Peter said. "I need to get up early and do things," he added. He'd be up early all right. He beamed from ear to ear with the thought of getting up at the crack of dawn and baking donuts. It was hard not to be excited for him. I wasn't sure if he could do it. However, I was wrong. Peter's donut shop outlasted and outlived all of us.

I helped Peter and Evelyn decorate the donut shop although we had to stay in a prescribed theme. We worked magic despite the restrictions. I had some extra time and energy and helped post signs and coupons around town and on the college campus. I'd do anything for Peter. Of course, I blame him for the daily habit I developed of having a single donut and coffee every day with my newspaper. For the next 30 years of my life I was at the donut shop every single morning barring a significantly icy snowstorm. It became my social connection and a meeting place for dozens of Greeley dwellers, old and young and somewhere in-between. It was a community center right in the heart of downtown Greeley and Peter happily made donuts every morning until his death at the ripe old age of 99.

Chapter 20

It's funny how fast time goes from 50 to 65. It's "boom" and you've reached retirement age. I've never really been sure what retirement means. I know I saved money and signed up for investments and pension programs that I offered the few employees I had. I felt it was important to their long-term security and my ability to keep them. Diana was still a youngster compared to Marvin and I. We sewed, finished and hung draperies for Diana until Marvin retired. Marvin and his wife sold their house in Greeley to the University for a handsome sum. It was a historic home that'd been in his family for a couple of generations, but needed significant restorative work. The two of them picked up and moved to the beach in South Carolina. We stayed in touch throughout our final years mostly by snail mail as most of us were not into the new computer age. I ran into Marvin's sons frequently at Peter's donut shop and kept up on the family's doings.

It's incredible how donuts and coffee bring people together. I'm not sure how word spread over the years, but Peter's donut shop grew in popularity constantly. I became a regular like many others, and we talked about each others' lives, wives, husbands, kids, death, disease, world peace – we discussed it all every day for an hour or two over donuts and coffee. Even if you pick up donuts and bring them to an office, people react. They hate them because they're fattening and unhealthy but they love the taste. For some reason people love donuts. It has to be the mix of bread and sugar. I love the sugar, bread and hint of fruit from the jelly. Mine were always jelly filled but without the powdered sugar because it was simply too messy!

I developed friendships with a financial investor, an internal medical specialist, nurses, and even college students. I helped one young man decide on a degree in interior design despite his parents' misgivings. I even got him a job with Diana on the weekends so he could learn the business inside and out. I tell you it was a community center with donuts – or the center of our community along with donuts and coffee! I made countless good friends and acquaintances. It served me well in the end and I even helped Peter out with the donuts on rare occasions when he wasn't quite up for the task. All in all, life was working out just fine as I was cresting over the hill and coming into the ripe old age of 70.

Everyday I got up early and walked with Ginger, and then we watched the news and headed down to the doughnut shop. Before noon we'd be in the basement working away. I worked about four hours and then if it were Friday, I'd head off down the street to look for garage sales. If I didn't find any I'd pull into the local Goodwill store and browse for bargains and treasures. No matter how old I got, I couldn't let go of the urge to decorate. I enjoyed shopping at thrift stores and garage sales looking for unique, or even antique items. Diana would come by every so often and check out my "stash." She'd buy some outright and I'd consign some in her shop. I made extra income and it gave me a reason to shop. I did love my shopping, more so when I was digging through "stuff" and looking for what I considered treasures. You'd be surprised at the things people throw away. I once found a picture frame of inlaid wood and ivory – selling that alone paid my bills for a year.

It was difficult to come to grips that I was retired. I was active, social, and enjoying my time immensely. I was by no means wealthy, but I had a comfortable savings, some small conservative investments, and was still making enough money monthly to pay my bills. My house was paid in full so outside of a few minor medical bills and Ginger's veterinary bills, I was in good shape financially. Ginger was aging rapidly it seemed but she lasted another year before I had to put her to sleep. It was one of the worst days of my entire life and I never could cope with getting another dog. So, I lived alone again outside of the wild rabbits in the backyard. Shortly after Ginger died, I quit walking. It lacked the joy it had held previously. Now my only exercise was heading downstairs to work and shopping.

After a short illness, Peter convinced me to get a checkup. We argued about it at the shop for months until I finally went in. I understood his paranoia, but just because his wife and two of his daughters had come up with breast cancer didn't mean I had it. I finally went to appease him.

I hadn't been in to see a doctor since I'd found out I couldn't have children so they needed to run every test known to medical science, or so it seemed. I thought about Evelyn and her two daughters. They'd all gone through chemotherapy treatment and one had a full mastectomy. The family had a rough time for a few years but fortunately they each made it through. Evelyn was still fragile, but she and Peter still lived near the farm so between Peter and the boys, they kept an eye on her. Well, after multiple appointments and several tests it was confirmed – I had it too. Breast cancer. I thought about what I wanted to do. I'd seen what Evelyn, Liz and Peter had to through They'd all had chemo treatments and surgeries. They'd all come through fine, but I'd watched them be sick and look horrible for weeks and months on end. I didn't want to go through all that, especially not alone. My breast cancer was not so severe that it was immediately life threatening, so I chose to let the tumors live.

I changed my diet to eat healthier, more greens and less red meat. Otherwise, I decided it would have to work itself out. Now, in hindsight perhaps the spinal tumors that killed me in the end wouldn't have existed if I had treated the breast tumors. However, I lived another fourteen years and that was plenty for me. I didn't tell anyone that my breast tumors were malignant. I told them the tumors were benign and didn't require treatment. Life went back to normal. I love normal.

Chapter 21

Let's go back and check in with how my twins were doing in California. It seemed to be the era of change and disease. There wasn't much time relax or let everything be normal as I'd hoped.

Dr. B and Liz lived in Monterey for several years until Dr. B was offered a position in San Francisco. He'd be the head medical director for a new hospital campus that served the city and northern California. It was an opportunity to reduce his medical hours while still being involved in patient care directly, but less often, and for a great deal more money. He could direct and manage the path the hospital would take. It was an exciting time for him. Liz was less than enthusiastic with the idea of moving. She had been working and moving up at the same bank for her entire career. She was the director of the mortgage division and considered an expert in home mortgage loans. It was quite impressive, or at least it was to me, her older sister.

We talked on the phone several times and she finally talked herself into transferring to a branch right in the center of downtown San Francisco's financial district. She was close to a full pensioned retirement so she accepted the transfer, albeit a bit testily. It was the only time I'd sensed tension between the two of them and it seemed to dissipate over time. It was completely forgotten when Liz was diagnosed with skin cancer the following year. Dr. B kept a close eye on the extensive sun damage on Liz's skin regularly from the first time they'd met and fortunately he'd seen a change early on. Liz underwent painful surgeries several times as they removed layers of damaged and cancerous cells. After they had the skin cancer under control, they found several tumors in her breasts. She had a full mastectomy and months of more chemotherapy.

I felt badly for her, as I myself spent time helping Peter and Evelyn get to their appointments for skin cancer tumors on his ears and her cheeks from so many seasons in the sun before sunscreen came along. Evelyn and Peter liked to get their appointments together and they couldn't drive after chemotherapy treatment, so I chauffeured them. It was the least I could do.

Liz's cancer seemed to stay around and relocate. Nearly every year from the time she turned 49 to 70 she was having another tumor treated or removed. It was enough to give one an ulcer, or activate the one you may already have, that's for sure. She ended up with significant scarring but no other complications. I'm not convinced that Liz's cancer ever went away at least not in my lifetime. Liz got so sick from the chemotherapy treatments that she eventually had to stop working. She joined me in the retirement ranks. Dr. B worked at least another ten years until he passed away a day after turning 70. Liz was crushed to say the least and an idea popped into my head. She could move back. She could move back with me and help me do Diana's curtain and detailing work.

I knew Liz didn't love San Francisco. It was cold for her, muggy, and overly crowded. Even though they lived in an upscale neighborhood she often mentioned feeling pinned in. The ocean was too cold to swim in without a wet suit and her sunbathing days were over. It took me a couple months, but I finally interjected into our reminiscing about Dr. B that very question. "Have you ever considered moving back to Greeley? Peter's doughnut shop is close and you could get a house that's more suited for you here." I'm not sure why I added the house part, I didn't know what her current home in San Francisco was like except it didn't have much of a yard. "Funny thing," she said, "Lois mentioned that very same thing just about a month ago. She's feeling superior now that she's been so healthy and her man is younger. I told her not to get too comfortable, but you know how she is," she said. I wasn't sure if that was a yes or a no, but it took me at least another two years to convince her.

I don't think it was me that convinced her in the end, it was Lois. Lois lived a fairly separate life from the rest of us. After the adoption revelation, she pulled even further away although I don't feel we judged her. Maybe we did, just not out loud. Lois lived with a man named Stewart. Stewart was a retired pilot when they'd met and Lois still worked at the corporate office in San Diego doing reservations. As the computer age took over, Lois wanted out. She retired at 67 rather than have to learn how to use one of those computer things as she put it. They both lived off generous pensions in a rented apartment and spent their extra time and money gambling and trying their luck at the nearby racetrack.

Stewart had two adult children who lived outside of San Diego. Both had joined the military and traveled back and forth depending on where they happened to be stationed and how long. Lois never got very close to anyone and they were no exception. Stewart spent time with his kids separately. Lois never minded. She'd pack up and take off for a week in Las Vegas or Reno, no problem at all. It seemed to work for them. Stewart was ten years older than Lois and passed away while traveling with his children to Yellowstone. Just like that, she had her own spacious apartment and was instantly lonely. Lois loved Stewart like a good, solid pet she'd never had. They got along well and enjoyed similar activities. Liz found out Stewart died six months after the fact when Lois stopped in for her usual bi-annual visit.

The fact that the three of us were alone came up and Lois worked to convince Liz to move back to Greeley. They decided they'd share a house together and called me. I wasted no time contacting a realtor I'd met at Peter's doughnut shop and he found them a home in less than a month. He even found a realtor in San Francisco to sell Liz's home. Liz made over 4 million dollars on the transaction! She was set for life. She had a pension, social security, and savings. They split the home purchase 50/50 and Liz paid all the bills. Their house was brand new and only six blocks away from mine. It was a ranch home with no stairs or basement. It had an attached garage with a small front and back yard. They came home late that summer and spent the first year planting trees, bushes, sod and flowers.

I was not much of an outdoor enthusiast so we met every morning at Peter's shop for doughnuts and coffee. The group welcomed them in and pretty soon the three of us became regular staples there. After awhile they seemed to settle into the routine of their childhood – wearing similar clothes and hairstyles. They colored each other's hair and styled it every week in swirled bouffant atop their heads. There was a short phase of the pixie haircut, but it didn't last long. Frequently, we'd leave the donut shop and I'd drive around and we'd go through garage sales looking for treasures. Liz refused to shop at the thrift stores, so we'd either go to the mall or I'd drop them off and pick them up when I was done at the thrift stores. Liz even took up painting for a couple years and their little home filled with artwork, then the garage filled, then the attic filled, and then she started giving them away and finally she stopped painting. Diana took a few into her store and Liz sold one or two every year. They weren't necessarily good, but they weren't bad either – the value of art really depends on one's taste.

The best one was of a large boat that she and Dr. B had in San Francisco. It sat anchored in a bay surrounded by a sunset. I had to admit that one was beautiful. Another one that was remarkable was a painting of her and Dr. B dancing the tango at the Top of the Mark in San Francisco. They'd gone twice a month to tango and have a drink with friends. Her face lit up and she got lost in it every time she looked at it.

Lois mostly gambled making routine trips to Las Vegas. She enjoyed gaming. I tried it a few times but was bored after thirty minutes. Lois could gamble and work those machines all day long and half the night. If you didn't insist she ate, she'd never take a break except to sip her white wine. We visited family every so often or they visited us. Together we attended weddings, funerals, baptisms, and birthday parties. Lois and Liz were always with a glass of white wine in one hand. Sometimes I'd just sit and watch them, thinking how far we'd all come since we took our breaks and played in that little creek as girls. We'd even tried to visit the farm, but it'd been commercialized and the creek became part of an office park. The sale of the farm provided income to our remaining brothers and their families, college educations and honeymoons for two generations. Peter remained the financial manager of the trust throughout his lifetime and he did a solid job.

Which brings us back to where we started, at my funeral. It was all peach and white, copper and orange. Damn cancer came back and ruined my spinal cord. I spent my last year in hospice barely able to move. It was a humbling experience overall, but a decent one all things considered. After a while nothing can be done for the pain of dying. It is simply painful. I gave away everything I could when I knew the deal was closing. I saw the tears in the eyes of my sisters, Peter, and the nieces and nephews I loved, which was more painful than the cancer. My nurses and I got along well, I shared my stories and they kindly listened. It takes a special human being to be a hospice nurse. My main nurse, Sandra even looked up photos of my designs on her computer. Diana had put them out on her website. There was my name on a computer. Amazing.

As I lay there that final afternoon, I watched the fireworks from my window, glistening bright yellow, gold and green. They went off over and over again little tiny bursts of light with no sound. I was mesmerized by the colors. I didn't hear the alarm sounding or the people rushing in. It was over as fast as it started, and I moved on.

Sandra was there in an instant followed by a doctor and a few other nurses. The notice to not resuscitate hung on my clipboard near the bed. Sandra took my pulse or confirmed I had none, and looked out the window wondering what I'd been watching. The only thing in the hospital courtyard was a hundred year old cottonwood, the sun glinting through the leaves as the wind blew. It sounded like a river rushing by. It'd proven calming to patients so they'd installed windows on all sides. There was a bird feeder that attracted any number of birds. Although, you couldn't hear them, they were fun to watch.

Working as a hospice nurse was a hard job but she had so many stories to tell from the people she'd cared for. Some day she was going to write them all down. For now, she smiled, kissed my forehead, dialed that final number and filled out the paperwork.

End